THE FRONTIERSMEN

Major Philip Gaunt and his former batman, Naik Alif Khan, veterans of dozens of skirmishes on British India's north-west frontier, are fighting the wild and dangerous land of northern Mexico. Aided by 'Buckskin' Carlson, a newly reformed drunk, they are hunting down Mexican bandidos who murdered the major's sister. But it proves to be a dangerous trail. Death by knife and gun is never far away. Will they finally deliver cold justice to the bandidos?

ELLIOT CONWAY

THE FRONTIERSMEN

Complete and Unabridged

LINFORD
Leicester

First published in Great Britain in 2004 by
Robert Hale Limited
London

First Linford Edition
published 2006
by arrangement with
Robert Hale Limited
London

The moral right of the author
has been asserted

British Library CIP Data

Conway, Elliot
   The frontiersmen.—Large print ed.—
   Linford western library
   1. Western stories
   2. Large type books
   I. Title
   823.9'14 [F]

   ISBN 1–84617–165–2

Published by
F. A. Thorpe (Publishing)
Anstey, Leicestershire

Set by Words & Graphics Ltd.
Anstey, Leicestershire
Printed and bound in Great Britain by
T. J. International Ltd., Padstow, Cornwall

This book is printed on acid-free paper

ULV - 03-02-06

For Claire and Simon Travers

1

Pat Mallon cracked the long bull-hide whip above the backs of the six-horse team. The horses snorted, kicked up dust belly high and the heavy Concorde stage, bouncing and swaying like a ship running before a high wind, picked up speed as it hit the foot of the long grade on the section of the Butterfield stage line south of the Big Dry Wash country of Arizona.

'You boys keep your eyes skinned!' he called out above the rattle of the stage. 'The murderin' sonsuvbitches slaughtered poor Stacey, his shotgun guard and his four passengers close by this stretch of the route.'

The two guards, one sitting alongside Mallon the other perched on the luggage rack facing their back-trail, tightened their grips on the double-barrelled shotguns, alert gazes flitting

1

every which way.

The first raid against the line was made against the stage making the east to west run, from St Louis, Missouri, to San Francisco, killing everyone on the stage. Such savage butchery was thought to have been the deadly work of a band of Apache, except that none of the victims had been scalped or mutilated and the raiders had been up on horses with iron-shod hooves.

The conclusion had been that the gang were Mexican *bandidos* who wanted to live long enough to enjoy their spoils by killing everyone who could at some possible time in the future finger them as road agents and sure candidates for a rope neck-tie. To give the driver the confidence to keep the line going, the Butterfield bosses had doubled the shotgun guards.

Santos, a stone-eyed, full-blood Mexican *bandido*, watched the stage come thundering up the grade from the rim of a wash not twenty feet from the trail. Then he switched his gaze westwards looking for the dust haze of riders lying back apiece on the trail, ready to come rib-kicking in to protect the stage if it came under attack. Santos could see no sign of any back-up guards, though he did notice the extra shotgun man on the stage. He cold-smiled. All it meant was that Tomas, the Yaqui 'breed, would have to arrow-shoot three men instead of two. Which wouldn't raise any sweat on Tomas who could flight a feathered stick as deadly accurate as any full-blood Yaqui.

Santos had planned the raids so that his gang would have all the edge. Using guns to put down the stage crew would have alerted the passengers they were under attack and, taking it that the male passengers would be armed, the stage could act as a small fort. A lengthy gunfight was something Santos didn't want. He was after easy pickings not getting his men needlessly shot down.

Tomas, on seeing the extra guard, stuck another arrow in the ground alongside the one already there. Then,

3

expressionless, he drew back on the arrow he had strung in his bow, aiming it at the rear guard. It was an easy kill, the team easing down almost to a gentle trot as they reached the head of the long hard pull.

The two men up on the front box didn't hear the rear guard's choking cough as the arrow pierced his throat, or see him roll off the roof of the stage dead before he hit the ground. Mallon cursed as he heard the clatter of the shotgun falling on to the footrest boards and the dead weight of the guard slumping against him. For one brief flash of time he thought that the guard had dozed off, then he saw the arrow deep in his chest and realized he had driven the stage into an ambush and it was too late to do anything about it.

Tomas's third shaft plunged between Mallon's ribs, piercing his heart, killing him dead, fast. The reins dropped out of his hands as he fell forward off his seat to land in a dust-raising thud, the stage leaving him behind, a crumpled bundle on the trail.

This time Santos's smile almost parted his lips. Tomas had done his killing business, now it was up to him and the rest of the *muchachos* and it seemed it was going to be another easy, no-risk raid. He drew his pistol and dug his spurs into his horse's ribs. The four road agents boiled out of the dry washes, pistols blazing. And without a shot being fired back at them a small massacre had taken place.

There had been four passengers on the stage, now lying bloodied and dead, crumpled against each other. While Tomas stood watch, the rest of the gang dragged the bodies out into the open and set about their grisly task of taking from the dead what money they carried and all that could be sold for hard cash. From one of the three male passengers, Santos not only got a gold timepiece but a cloth money-belt heavy with coins that had been strapped across his belly under his shirt. In a jacket pocket he discovered two packs of playing-cards with the seals unbroken.

Wide-grinning now, he said, 'We've struck gold here, *amigos*! This gamblin' man has played his last game of poker and lost!'

Santos looked down at the body of the only woman passenger. A fine-looking female, he thought. It was a shame that she had to be killed; she was still young and strong enough to bring a good price selling her to some Apache or Yaqui chief, after he'd had his pleasure with her. Though the two rings he took off her right hand and the gold chain hanging round her neck did make up somewhat for his disappointment. Santos didn't doubt that they would find further rich pickings when they went through her cases.

Within twenty minutes of Tomas loosing off his first death-dealing arrow, the *bandidos* had mounted up and were ready to head south to the Mexican border, driving before them the six stage horses to ride over ground on which a fully laden Conestoga would not show signs of its passing.

Only when the trail dust of the raiders had been lost to his gaze in the shimmering heatwaves did the old drifter known in the territory as Buckskin Jake Carlson, come round from the tumble of rocks he had been sheltering behind to close-eye the merciless killings he had watched taking place.

The bloody sight caused Buckskin to double up as though in pain and throw up, drawing the rotgut whiskey out of his system making him as sober as a Jesuit priest. On walking up to the girl's body, Buckskin wished he had still been drunk.

Buckskin lived some sort of an existence here in the badlands of the Big Dry territory, on what he could trap and his regular whiskey intake, as he searched for the lost Spanish gold and silver mines he believed had been dug in the valleys and canyons in the hills behind him. Occasionally, he supplemented his rations by selling wolf skins in Bitter Water Creek, the nearest town. Knowing that the east-bound stage came to almost a walking pace when it reached the head of the long haul of the pass, he had hoped to beg a bottle of whiskey from the driver or his shotgun guard before the horses came under the whip again.

He had seen the five riders coming up from the border. As they came closer, Buckskin could see that the men were double armed so he ruled them out as being hard working *vaqueros*. He heard their leader, a small hatchet-faced Mexican shout out some orders and the men went to ground on both sides of the trail. He had no doubts now he was seeing an ambush set up for the Butterfield stage. Panic stricken, he moved further back among the rocks wrapping his dirty bandanna round his mule's nose to stop it from braying when it caught the smell of the *bandidos*' horses, or he would have ended up as dead as the poor folk he was looking down on.

Buckskin knew what had to be done though he was doubtful that he had the strength to do it. He couldn't make it to Bitter Water Creek in under two hours, the speed his old mule moved at, even being rib-kicked all the way there and another hour for a posse to be raised and get back here. In that time what the buzzards, already circling over head, and the four-legged carrion-seekers would do to the pretty lady's body chilled Buckskin's blood and gave him the strength to dig the graves.

They would not be the regular six-feet deep Boot Hill graves but deep enough to protect the bodies until a priest conducted hymn-singing funerals. He walked back to his mule for the spade strapped on its back and kept casting anxious glances over his shoulder for any sign of the hell riders coming back. He chose a piece of ground close to the bodies for the graves. Taking off his tattered hide coat he began to dig into the soft sandy soil with a craving for several pulls at a bottle of whiskey that screamed in his brain.

2

Major Philip Gaunt looked down from the balcony window of his hotel at the colourful and noisy crowd below him. He had been led to believe that St Louis, Missouri, was the gateway for Americans seeking their fortunes in the vast, mainly unmapped lands of the far West. By the shouting and to-and-froing, the would-be fortune seekers seemed to him to be in one damned hurry to begin looking for their hoped-for future riches.

He saw men of all shades of colour, from the jet black of the stripped-to-the-waist muscular Negroes loading bales of cotton on to a moored paddle-steamer, the browns of the head-feathered Indians, and men of Spanish blood who wore high-steepled hats and jangling, sawtoothed spurs, to the blue-uniform detail of white-faced soldiers being shepherded through the press by a bellowing sergeant.

Then the major's eye caught sight of several men, favouring wild, untrimmed, shaggy beards wearing long-skirted hide coats and armed with long rifles, walking with a proud confident purpose in their stride. Hunters, trappers, the major thought, or, as their countrymen called them, frontiersmen.

Philip thin-smiled. His former orderly, Naik Alif Khan, could walk alongside them and not seem out of place, though the tall, hawk-faced Afridi corporal's frontier was thousands of miles away, stretching hundreds of miles across the arid, rocky, bloodstained land between British India and Afghanistan.

It had once been his frontier. Then he had been the CO of a company of Afridi Riflemen, like his father and grandfather before him. It had been the Rifles' operating task to seek out and destroy the Mashud and Wazri lashkars, war-bands, killing villagers who lived under the protection of the British Raj. The Afridis he commanded were every bit as bloodthirsty as the warriors they were hunting down, but they had taken the Raj's salt and gold and their *Pakhtunwali*, their code of honour, committed them to fight to their last drop of blood to uphold the Raj's law and protect the life of their major *sahib*.

Again, a cold reflective smile came on the major's face. His wild ruffians had done just that. Their fierce bravado, be it in attack against a bandit hill fort, or fighting their way out of an ambush, had saved him many times from ending up stretched on some *khud* side having his privates removed, while still alive, by some Wazri women, every bit as fierce as their menfolk.

Eighteen months ago, on a normal routine patrol, a lone sniper, tribe unknown, picking him out as an officer *sahib*, shot him in the right leg. The round from the sniper's *jezail*, a pass-made rifle, was more like a lump of lead than a machine-turned cartridge and did that much more damage. Alif and three of his squad rigged up a rough stretcher and practically ran nonstop in the blistering heat across ground a mountain goat would look twice at before placing its feet, to a British fort with a military doctor on its muster roll. The speed at which his men had got him to specialist medical aid had prevented him from losing his leg.

In spite of his limb having been saved, the major had still had to resign his commission in the Frontier Rifles. The painful stiffness in his leg, which he knew he would carry to the grave, meant that he could no longer cope with the punishing strain of forced marches across razor-backed ridges and the sliding shale slopes of the frontier territory.

Being country born, he returned to an England he had never seen before to make a complete break with the regiment. The major knew that Alif was embroiled in some bloody inter-family feud and not wanting a man he counted as his blood brother to end up with his throat cut in some lonely pass when he was no longer with the regiment, he asked the big Afridi to accompany him to England as his batman. It would keep Alif alive without him losing face.

They had been in England three months when the major received the invite from some friends of the family holidaying in America, to join them on a hunting trip they were organizing in the State of Montana. Philip grabbed the offer with both hands; the damp English spring was playing hell with his wounded leg, and, he guessed, though he hadn't said so, that Alif didn't find the English climate to his taste.

'Some relatives of mine, Alif,' he said, 'have learned that I have resigned my commission and I'm now living in the family home and have asked me to join their hunting party in Montana. They write that it is good hunting country, teeming with bear, mountain lions and deer.' He grinned at Alif. 'And is inhabited by wild Indians. I would be grateful if you would accompany me to look after my guns and horses. And if we bump into any of those wild Indians an extra rifle won't come amiss.'

The 'wild' Indians puzzled Alif more than somewhat. The Indians he had come across were anything but wild. They had been infidel Hindu shop-keepers in the bazaars of Lahore and soft-bellied Brahmin moneylenders.

Po-faced, Alif said, 'I would like to meet some of these wild Indians, Major *sahib*. See if they are as wild as the Mashuds and the Wazris. And find out if they die just as easily when Allah places them in the sights of my Snider. I will start packing, *Sahib*.'

Philip grinned inwardly. He had seen the gleam in Alif's eyes. 'You do that, Alif,' he replied. 'There is a whole pile of letters to write and forms to fill in, orderly clerk's work by Jove, before we leave for America.'

There was another reason why Philip had taken up the offer of joining the hunting trip. His younger sister Jennifer, whom he had never seen since she had left India as a child to attend school in England, then decided to make her life there, would be in America the same time he was. The ship she was passenger on was due to dock at San Francisco in two months' time on the last but one leg of her whirlwind trip around the world. In a letter to her great aunt, whom she lived with, Jennifer, told of how, to see as much of America as she could, she was going to book passage on the Butterfield stage line that ran a service stretching 2,600 miles, across five or six states to journey's end at St Louis, Missouri.

The major smiled. If Jennifer had been a man, she could have made an excellent company commander in the Rifles. By the odd letter she had penned to him while he was with the regiment he had discovered that she had a yearning thirst for travel and adventure, for visiting outlandish places

17

a well-brought-up young lady should not be even interested in. She would get a surprise, Philip thought, when she saw her brother waiting to greet her as she stepped off the stagecoach at St Louis. It had been twenty-three years since they had last set eyes on each other. Now he was in St Louis. The major pulled out his watch and glanced at the time. The stage office should be open so he would be able to find the exact date and time Jennifer's stage would arrive. He smiled as he walked along the street to the office. Jennifer might change whatever other travel plans she had made and join him on the hunting trip.

★ ★ ★

A half-hour later, Major Gaunt came out of the depot office his Indian sun-bronzed face unusually pale and drawn, a thousand-yard stare in his eyes. The ominous words, 'I have to regretfully inform you, Major Gaunt, that your sister is dead,' from the depot manager echoing like the bells of Hell in his ears.

He had jerked up straight in his chair when Mr Laing, the depot manager, told him of Jennifer's death. He leaned forward and gripped the edge of the manager's desk so hard his knuckles cracked.

'How did she die?' he asked, in a rasping voice.

As the manager related the fearful manner of his sister's death his shocked-looking face boned over. And Mr Laing found he was no longer addressing a quiet-spoken English officer and a gentleman. He had seen that cold, seething, yet controlled rage on Apache broncos' faces when being dragged back to the agency in chains by an army detail. He could taste the anger the major was feeling and it scared him no end.

'Head office did send a letter to a Mrs Clara Gaunt at an address in England informing her of the tragedy.

We got the address from a letter we found in her coat,' the manager added, head down, not having the nerve to meet that gut-weakening gaze.

'Have the authorities apprehended those, those *bandidos?*' Philip said, voice as hard as his face.

'I-I really don't know, Major,' Laing stammered, shaken by the English officer's penetrating look. 'The Butterfield directors are putting pressure on the state marshals and the army in Arizona not to spare men or expense to hunt down the gang, but it's big wild territory out there and is home to dozens of such like gangs of thieves and killers. Then there's the renegade Indians doing their share of killing and stealing. The man you need to contact for the latest information regarding the apprehension of the gang is Marshal Brodwell, the peace officer at Bitter Water Creek, Arizona.' Laing cleared his throat nervously. 'Your sister is buried there.' Meeting Philip's eyes for the first time he said, firm-voiced, 'I have been instructed by the company to give you any assistance you may ask for, Major Gaunt.'

Without any hesitation Philip said, 'There is something you can do for me right now, Mr Laing, and I would appreciate it if you would treat my request with some urgency. Book me a passage on the fastest transport that will get me to this Bitter Water Creek.' Philip thin-smiled. 'No expense to be spared. I hope to hear from you within the hour.' He gave Laing a curt nod before turning and leaving the office. Behind him, Laing began to write out a sheaf of Western Union flimsies frantically and yell for the office junior to get his lazy ass in here pronto.

By the time he had made the short walk back to his hotel, Philip's mind was clear enough to begin to think like the officer he was. It wasn't as though it was a military campaign he had decided to embark on, more of a settling of a blood feud, but he knew that feuds were not ended without a great deal of bloodshed and killing. He would have to think coolly and logically. He would be one man against five or six men as cunning and as vicious as any tribesman he had fought against. And like the men of the North-West hills they had the advantage of knowing the ground they operated on. It would be a family feud so he could not call on Alif's help.

Alif was sitting cleaning and oiling the shotguns and the large-bore hunting rifles when the major came into his room. Alif had only once seen that grim look of desperation on his major's face. It had been when a patrol of the Rifles had been pinned down for four hours on a barren hillside under a blazing sun by a band of Afghans, suffering heavy casualties.

Suddenly, they had heard the major shout, 'Do we go to Paradise like dogs or warriors?' then he had leapt to his feet and charged up the hillside firing his pistol. The rest of the patrol, knives drawn, had followed him, screaming their war cries, sweeping the surprised Afghans off the ridge, killing all who stood and fought.

Now, he laid down the cleaning cloths and got to his feet. '*Sahib?*' he asked, a questioning look in his eyes.

'Fearful news, my old friend, fearful news,' the major grated. 'Miss Jennifer has been killed by *badmash*. It is my duty to hunt down the bandits. And being this is my own family's business I have no right to ask you to risk your life in an affair that is of no concern to you, Alif. I will arrange for your passage back to England and you're more than welcome to stay at my house.' He favoured Alif with a wry smile. 'Look after things until I return.'

Alif drew himself up to his full six feet two inches, looking down his nose at Philip.

'Major *sahib*,' he said. 'I have obeyed thy commands for fifteen years, this order I will not obey.' Then Alif seemed to grow a few extra inches, towering over Philip. 'We of the Rifles have shed blood for each other,' he said. 'A hurt against one is a hurt against all. These *feringhi* dogs who have killed your kin have dishonoured all of us. An insult that can only be wiped out by their blood. My *Pakhtunwali* to the Rifles binds me to be at thy side, Major *sahib*, and help thee to take that blood.'

Philip's black mood lifted somewhat. The odds of avenging his sister's death were swinging more in his favour. 'I will glady accept thy rifle and dagger alongside mine, Naik Alif Khan. It was remiss of me not to have asked you to accompany me. Please accept my apologies. Now we are going to face great odds, Alif, and it would be foolish not to arm ourselves accordingly. We will leave the hunting guns here at the hotel and buy ourselves some faster firing power rifles than your Snider and my Lee-Metford. The American Winchester repeating rifles should be ideal weapons . . . ' Philip smiled. 'Why on earth am I dicussing the merits of rifles with you, Alif? You cut your damn teeth on a rifle barrel. Choose what guns you think best. I'll go back to the stage office and book an extra seat to this Bitter Water Creek.'

3

It had been a long, impatient journey to Bitter Water Creek for the major though most of the travelling had been done by rail. On leaving the train at the depot in Arizona he had hired a private stage for the trip south to his destination. Cal Lewis, the stage driver, had been more than a mite surprised that his two passengers opted to sit on top rather than inside of the stage. The English dude who had hired the stage, dressed in some sort of a lightweight uniform and wearing a basin-shaped hat with a cloth attached to it to protect the wearer's neck from the sun, sat alongside him, nursing a fourteen-load Winchester across his knees. To give the limey dude his due, he just sat there, po-faced, swallowing the dust and getting jerked and bounced to hell and back without even a murmur of complaint.

His hawk-visaged buddy had perched himself on the luggage rack holding a cannon of a rifle that could blow a buffalo apart at 500 yards. His garb was just as outlandish. A long nightshirt, baggy pants and a few feet of cloth wrapped around his head serving as a hat. Cal couldn't make up his mind what race or tribe the big rangy man belonged to.

Cal had the urge to ask the dude why he was paying him good money to get him to Bitter Water Creek, with, as he put it, great despatch, but he didn't want to ask nosy questions that could upset the mean-looking son-of-a-bitch behind him. Though Cal knew for certain, by the pair's Indian-faced expressions and the four brand-new Winchester repeaters and belts of reloads stored aboard with the rest of their gear, big trouble was coming soon for someone Bitter Water Creek ways.

Cal drew up the team in the corral of the stage depot and kicked on the coach brake. 'Journey's end. As you can see it ain't much of a town, so I reckon it won't boast a hotel, but there oughta be a roomin'-house on Main Street.'

'We won't be in town long enough to want a hotel, Mr Lewis,' the major replied. 'Once I have had words with the town's marshal, a Mr Bradwell so I have been told, and we get horses and supplies, we'll be riding further west.' His dust-caked face cracked in a white-toothed smile. 'I have had more comfortable journeys, Mr Lewis, but you fulfilled my orders by making excellent time getting us here.'

Then Philip told Alif to unload their kit and watch over it until he returned from seeing the marshal.

Marshal Bradwell met him on the porch of his office. 'I've been expecting you, Major Gaunt. I had a wire from St Louis statin' you were on your way. I know you'll be in need of a bath and some hot food, but I figure you'll want to see your sister's grave first. Can you ride, Major?'

'You are right, Marshal,' replied the major. 'I do want to see my sister's grave.' He smiled. 'And I can ride, if you can supply me with a mount.'

'No problem,' the marshal said. 'My deputy's horse is across at the livery barn havin' a shoe seen to, it should be ready by now. I'll saddle it up and have it standin' here in about fifteen minutes.'

'That will do fine,' replied Philip. 'It will give me time to tell my companion I will be away for a while.'

★　★　★

'This is where your sister is buried, Major,' Marshal Bradwell said. 'My wife didn't think that the town's Boot Hill was a fittin' place for a fine English lady to be laid to rest in. It is my family's buryin' plot. My pa and ma and a boy of mine rest there.'

A sombre-faced Major Gaunt took in the small, white-painted fenced enclosure shaded by a clump of sweeping branched oaks. The grass was neatly trimmed with bunches of wild flowers growing through. Time had not allowed nature to cover Jennifer's grave, it was still a stark oblong of brown earth and stones. Though, he noticed, someone in the marshal's family had placed a vase of flowers on the grave and fixed a dressed wooden cross at its head.

The major gave a slow nod of satisfaction before turning and facing the lawman.

'Marshal Bradwell,' he said, 'your good lady has done me a great service, given me peace of mind and I will be forever in your family's debt. I had intended to take my sister's body back to England to be buried in the family vault but I couldn't have wished for a more pleasant spot for my sister's resting place.' Philip eyed the marshal's cabin and the outbuildings. 'I take it, of course, you and your family are settled here permanently.'

'My grandpa built that shack, Major,' the marshal replied. 'He died in it, so did my pa and I hope to do likewise.' He grinned. 'But not for quite a spell yet. I ain't reckonin to be wearin' a peace-officer's badge till I'm too old to haul myself up on to a horse. As soon as I've raised enough capital I'm goin' to run cattle and horses here, I own a good patch of sweet grass. Now, if you're ready to ride back to town, I'll give you all the information I've got on that bunch of murderers who killed your sister.' The marshal gave the major a close-eyed look. 'I'm not jumpin' the gun thinkin' that you've got your mind on huntin' down those *bandidos*, Major?'

Philip gave the marshal a smile that held no warmth in it at all. 'You would be thinking correctly,' he said, as he swung up into his saddle. And left it at that. A great weight had been lifted from his shoulders. Jennifer had been decently buried. Now all his thoughts could be concentrated on the hunt for her killers. He dug his heels into his horse's ribs.

On the ride back to Bitter Water Creek, knowing that the major had a lot on his mind, the marshal held his peace. It wasn't his business to tell a man, an officer to boot, that the course of action he was about to set on could get him a plot alongside his sister.

He gave the major a long studying look. He hadn't met an Englishman before. At first glance, being a medium built man, this one had nothing to set him apart from a Yankee dude but his accent. Except the hard, penetrating-eyed look he had given him when he had spoken to him about his tracking down of the killers. The marshal recollected seeing such-like looks coming from the hell-raiser, Jeb Stuart, the horse soldier Reb general, during the War. Maybe, just maybe, the marshal thought, he was selling the major short.

Marshal Bradwell and the major dismounted outside the marshal's office, the major asking for all the intelligence he had on the bandits before the lawman had taken his left foot out of his stirrup iron. For a dude, the marshal thought, the major was one hell of a fire cracker. He could see the tiredness etched in deep lines on his face and he wasn't giving a damn about getting himself cleaned up. He was in one big hurry to get on the trail of his sister's killers. The marshal was beginning to get an inkling of the strength of the major's character, comparing him once again with the wild-ass Jeb Stuart.

'We know what the bastards look like,' the marshal began. 'Leastways . . . ' Then he broke off with a gasped, 'Who the hell's that frightenin' *hombre*?'

Philip swung round to see Alif coming towards them. 'Why, that is my one-time batman, Marshal, an Afridi,' he said. Then, grim-smiling, he said, 'Once I commanded a hundred and fifty of such warriors, warring against men every bit as brutal and efficient in their killing ways and in a land that makes your bailiwick look like the Garden of Eden. So you see, my friend,

I am not what you Westerners call a greenhorn in matters concerning the hunting down of men. I am not letting my grief at the death of my sister cloud my military judgement, or indeed underestimate the enormity and danger of the task I have set myself.'

The major introduced Alif to Marshal Bradwell. 'The marshal and his family kindly saw that Jennifer was decently buried and I have decided not to take her body back home. Now we can get on with the business at hand.'

Alif gave the lawman a curt nod of greeting, Bradwell reciprocating as he wondered who would scare him more, being jumped by an Apache or an Afridi.

Eyeing the the long gun and the horse soldier sabre-like knife Alif was armed with, Seth thought that the major must have some special powers to be able to boss over 150 cut-throat wild men. Though it was his duty to alert the major to the dangers he could be facing out there in the border territory.

'Major,' he said, 'I oughta warn you that you could run into extra trouble down there in the badlands along the Mex border. Real bad trouble, Apache trouble.' Seth grinned. 'But I figure you know your trade. You haven't come all this way just to hear me preach to you, Major. Let's go and have words with old Buckskin.' Seth's face hardened. 'He saw the raid on the stage.'

'Buckskin?' queried Philip.

'Buckskin Jake Carlson,' the marshal said. 'A ragged-assed drifter. Spends his time scratting around the territory searchin' for old Spanish silver mines he reckons are in the hills west of here. When he runs out of liquor and other supplies, he hauls himself back to Bitter Water Creek to do odd jobs to raise himself a few dollars to build up his supplies again, especially his liquid rations. He should be replenishin' his intake of whiskey at Peake's bar just across the street there.'

'Drunk, you say, Marshal?' Philip said. He grinned at Alif. 'I think it calls for the 'treatment', old friend.'

'The 'treatment'?' repeated the marshal.

'We suffered with the odd drunk in the company, Marshal,' Philip replied. 'And I mean a man so inflamed with native distilled liquor he would have embarked on a massacre in the company lines if he had not been restrained. Alif would sober him up pretty damn quick, to keep the trouble in the family so to speak.'

The 'treatment' would have to be good, the marshal thought, as he led the major and Alif across to the bar. He couldn't see the old whiskey soak running amok threatening the citizens of Bitter Water Creek with a pig sticker, but he had been an on-and-off drunk for nigh on three years.

'There he is, Major,' he said, as they stepped through the bar doors, pointing to a figure slumped across a table near the bar.

Peake wondered why the marshal was bringing a weird-dressed, hair-lifting, red son-of-a-bitch into his bar and was angry enough to tell him to kick his ass off his premises, when the red son-of-a-bitch favoured him with a hair-lifting look that dried up his angry words and made him wish he was someplace else.

The major looked down at the only link to the killers of his sister. A drunken old man, unkempt-haired, wearing clothes that would not look out of place on the back of a bazaar beggar. His shoulders sagged briefly thinking of the enormity of the task he had set himself. Then his lips thinned into hard, determined lines. He had to work with the material at hand; it did no good wishing otherwise.

'Alif,' he snapped, 'let us begin sobering up Mr Carlson. Get him where we can give him a much needed cold plunge or two.' He called across to Peake standing open-mouthed behind his bar, 'I would be obliged if you can give me a big jug of heavily salted water and the same of coffee, black and strong.'

'You do that, Peake,' the marshal said, then he watched Alif reach down and hoist Buckskin's inert body over his left shoulder as effortlessly as a man picking up a baby. 'This I want to see. Follow me, big fellow, there's a horse-waterin' tank just along the street.'

By the time the major came up to the tank carrying the two jugs, Buckskin had come to.

Dripping wet, unsteady-legged and spluttering curses like a mule-skinner, Buckskin tried to focus his alcohol-dulled brain on just who the hell was doing this to him. Then his bleary-eyed gaze caught sight of a fierce, brown-skinned face and his stomach heaved. How the hell had the Apache taken him from Peake's bar? Had he wandered out of town when he was pie-eyed drunk and staggered into the arms of a war band? And why were the red sons-of-bitches trying to drown him instead of roasting him over a small fire?

Before he could reason through his predicament, Buckskin felt himself being lifted up by the big Apache and dropped into the water again.

This time when he was dragged out of the water he thought he saw the town marshal and, still fuddle-brained, he opined that the Apache must have captured him as well. If so, why was the lawman smiling fit to bust? Then Buckskin had no more time for trying to think things through for the Apache had gripped him again and liquid was being poured down his throat. He tasted salt, heaps of it in the water, the red devils were going to stake him out to let him die of thirst. He gagged and tried to break out of the Apache's vice-like grip but still the salt water was being poured into him.

Then Buckskin began to retch. Alif grunted and released his hold of his victim and stepped clear. Buckskin threw up until he was too weak to keep his balance. He sank slowly to the ground, certain that the blackness overwhelming him was welcome death.

When Buckskin regained his senses it wasn't Hell he had found himself in but the marshal's office sitting in a chair with a blanket draped over his shoulders holding his fourth cup of coffee that tasted like roof pitch in hands that shook. He had thrown up and was now about to piss out most of the alcohol in his system.

His brain and vision had cleared enough for him to see that the bastard who had been dumping him in the tank was too hairy-faced to be an Apache. Though he had the stone-eyed mean visage to pass as a hair-lifting buck. He had regained enough of his courage to give him a mean look of his own. The white man wearing some sort of a uniform, standing next to the marshal, also had him puzzled, though he judged he was the big ape's boss.

He struggled up on to his feet. 'What the hell's-goin' on, Marshal?' he cried. 'That Injun-lookin' asshole almost drowned me!' He glared angrily at Philip. 'I oughta sue you for assault, mister. I may do once I get back to Peake's bar and get my clothes dried, bein' these are all I have — and get a drink if I've got a stomach to hold any liquor.'

'I'm sorry for the way you have been treated, Mr Carlson,' the major replied. 'But it was important that I sobered you up, fast. I'm Major Gaunt and I would appreciate it if you would tell me about the raid on the Butterfield stage you witnessed. How many of them there were, descriptions, in which direction did they ride off after the raid; everything you can remember about them. It is very important to me, for the girl you saw killed was my sister.'

Buckskin's anger rapidly cooled. 'I'm right sorry to hear that, Major,' he said. 'But I told the marshal all about the raid. And I've been hittin' the whiskey real hard since the killin's. I can't remember what day it is. So I can be no more help to you.'

41

'Oh, you can still be of help to me,' the major said. 'A great help. You know what the killers look like. I intend hunting them down. You, if you ride with me, can identify them.'

'Me! Ride with you?' Buckskin sank back into the chair, his eyes rolling wildly. 'Just . . . just you and your Injun-lookin' pard?' He looked at the marshal. 'Tell him what's out there, Marshal. Tell him about Geronimo and his Apache wild boys, tell him about the other Mex *bandidos* and our own home-grown cut-throats who murder and steal in that territory. No offence, Major, but by your manner of speakin' I figure you for an English dude; the land itself will prove too much for you to tackle.'

'No offence taken,' replied the major. 'I do know what will be facing us in that wild territory. Alif Khan' — he smiled at Buckskin — 'my *Indian-looking pard*, and myself were soldiers in the British Army serving in India and we have had more than our fair share of fighting against men just as forbidding as any you have knowledge of, in a land no more hospitable. But you will be able to aid us to move faster across it by showing us the passes through the mountains, and where we can expect to find water.' The major's smile chilled over. 'When it comes to the reckoning, well that will be mine and Alif's business. I am hiring you as a guide, nothing more. Naturally I will pay you, and supply you with all you require for the hunt — horse, weapons and clothes. What say you, Mr Carlson?'

A more-or-less sober Buckskin did some fast but deep thinking. His aching joints told him he was getting too old to be out there in the heat and the goddamned ball-freezing nights digging for what he knew was a lost cause. Cash in hand and new gear wouldn't come amiss, he thought. And it wasn't as though he had to do any fighting if they did come up with the hundred-in-one chance of meeting up with the killers. The dude major had said that he hadn't been hired to do any shootin'. There was the possibilty of running into Geronimo but that red son-of-a-bitch could be in his hole-up in the Sierra Madre down there in old Mexico. In any case, he didn't think the major's 'hunt' would last more than a week or so; cold rough camps would quickly dampen his keenness to track down his sister's killers. Every way he looked at it, gave him the chance to die with his boots off at a very old age, in comfort.

What had finally swayed Buckskin's mind to take up the major's offer was the sneering look the big, hatchet-faced Alif was giving him. He was gazing at him as though he was a pile of buffalo chips. Which, he admitted, was a fair observation. A tiny spark of pride flickered in Buckskin's chest. By thunder, he thought, he would show them that he hadn't drunk all his balls away.

'I'll be your guide, Major,' he said. 'Though that ain't a promise I can lead you to those killers you're huntin'.'

Buckskin managed a smile, the first for a very, very long time. 'But you can bet on it that you won't want for water.'

The major gave a relieved smile. 'We can but try, Mr Carlson. We can but try. Now we can start gathering together what we need, Alif, horses first; you can get what clothes, weapons, etc. that you require, Mr Carlson. I want everything ready for moving out just after dawn.'

Zeke Burke, owner of the livery barn, thought he could unload several of his old, broken-winded horses on to the English dude, though he quickly changed his mind when he saw the 'dude' examining the horses with the expertise of a man who knew the finer points of horse flesh. And it looked as though he was passing his opinion of the horses, in some heathen language, to his big, ugly-looking partner.

The major smiled inwardly. The old rogue of a horse trader couldn't even fool him regarding the fitness of the horses he was trying to sell him. He certainly couldn't hoodwink Alif, who came from a long line of Afridi horse-stealers.

'Alif,' he said in Pushtu. 'We haven't the time to stand here and haggle as though we are in some Kashmiri bazaar, give that thief a 'we-mean-business' look.'

Alif drew back his upper lip in a wolf-like snarl and glared at Zeke, dropping his hand on to the hilt of his big Afghan knife as he did so.

Alif's ploy worked. Zeke got the message that his underhanded dealing was liable to heap a load of grief on to him. He favoured his customers with a weak smile. 'I've some other stock more suitable to your requirements, gents, in the corral out back.' Zeke suddenly cast an alarmed glance over the major's shoulder and the major heard a muttered, 'Well I'll be damned!'

The major swung round just in time to see the backs of three riders passing the alley entrance. He looked back at Zeke. 'Trouble?' he said.

Zeke nodded. 'Big trouble, for the marshal. Bein' you seem new to the territory, I reckon you ain't familiar with the takin' ways of the Clancey brothers. Well, the whole clan, includin' their late pa, are in the cattle-stealin' business. They work out of a hole-up in the badlands just this side of the Mex border. Last week the marshal shot dead Carson Clancey, the eldest brother, when the boys tried to lift cows from a nearby ranch. You've just seen Ned, Bubba and Newt ridin' in to even up the score.'

'Can't the marshal call on any support?' the major asked.

'Nah,' replied Zeke. 'When the Clanceys show up in town, folks tend to lock and bolt their doors and keep low till the Clanceys ride out again.

The major shot a significant glance at Alif. Alif replied with a blood-chilling grin and hefted the Snider.

Zeke understood the looks. He gave them both a disbelieving stare. 'You ain't about to side with the marshal agin those three *pistoleros*, are you, gents?'

'I owe the marshal a big favour,' replied the major. 'In the meanwhile, I would be obliged if you could pick me out three saddle horses and two pack animals, and all their tack.' The major gave Zeke a no-nonsense look. 'The best you have, understand?'

'I'll do that, mister,' said Zeke. 'You'll not find finer stock in the whole of the territory.' Then he thought that the favour the dude reckoned he owed the marshal could get him and his big pard killed. And he would be giving himself a lot of work for damn all recompense as dead men don't pay their bills.

Marshal Bradwell locked his office door, Bitter Water Creek not being a trail town there was no need for him to patrol it at night to calm down any out-of-hand rowdiness from trail hands in the town's two saloons. He stepped off the boardwalk and loosened his mount's reins from the hitching post. As he put a foot into the stirrup iron he saw the Clancey brothers, wide-faced grinning at him from across the street. A chill of fear swept over him, his grand dreams of running a horse ranch were going to end right here in blood and pain for not realizing the Clanceys would act swiftly to avenge their brother's death.

The marshal nudged his horse away from him so he had clear view of his would-be executioners.

'Well, boys,' he said, more bold than he was feeling. 'You've sure got me by the balls. Though I see it's taken three of you to do it. I figure I'm fast enough to down one of you so he can meet up with that asshole, Carson, before the two of you that's left do for me.'

'And which one would that be, Marshal Bradwell?' Philip called out. 'For Alif and I will, as you put it, down the remaining two assholes.'

Four pairs of eyes swivelled left and right and hands that were inching towards holstered pistols stayed their movement. And only Marshal Bradwell was smiling as he took in the ramrod-backed figure of the major standing to the left of the Clanceys, a pistol held loosely down the right leg of his pants. On the other side of the Clanceys was the imposing sight of the barn-sized Alif, his fancy-worked rifle held across his chest. Seth could have kissed them both.

The Clanceys, all their overpowering edge gone, stood there frozen, uncertain of their next moves, faces showing their angry fear. All wondering what type of men the marshal had hired as his deputies.

Alif barked something in Pushtu that the marshal saw brought a smile to the major's face.

'My companion asks, Marshal Bradwell,' the major said, 'if all the so-called men in this land of yours fight like cowardly pi-dogs, only having the courage to attack their victim in a pack.'

Ned Clancey was the first of the clan to be stung by the insult. With face working in mad-eyed rage, flecks of spittle bubbling at the corners of his mouth as he cursed and swore, he grabbed for his pistol.

The two rapid echoing cracks of the five-load Webley held by the major at arm's length were deadened by the loud bang of the Snider's discharge. And Ned was the first of the Clanceys to die as a Webley shell pierced the left temple, exiting in a grisly splatter of blood and bone. The Webley's second round was also a fast-killing shot, tearing into Bubba's heart and dropping him to the ground alongside Ned.

The heavy Snider slug also did its deadly work, hammering into Newt's upper body with sledgehammer force, whirling him round, arms outflung, as though caught by a small, invisible twister. He staggered back several paces, pain and the puzzlement of how the hell had he and his brothers walked into this crap situation flickering across his face before folding up in the middle and raising dust spouts on Main Street as he hit the ground.

The marshal let out his breath in a long, low hiss of relief. He had never seen such fast, professional killing. He had his gun fisted, but, like the now dead Clanceys, he hadn't fired a shot. There wouldn't be two greenhorns going hunting for the stage *bandidos* but two *hombres* well versed in the killing business. Arizona, New Mexico with its bronco Apache, Gringo and Mex *pistoleros* was a wild frontier, but the marshal believed it paled against the frontier the major and his big plug-ugly pard once soldiered in.

'Major,' he said, as he walked across the street towards them. 'Those bastards sure had me between one helluva rock and a hard place. I'm beholden to both of you for savin' my life.'

'Think nothing of it, Marshal,' the major replied. 'It is I who is beholden to you. You took care of my sister's body. What Alif and I did was what we are trained to do. Indeed, often we had to fight small battles.'

'Yeah, well, whatever,' replied the

marshal. 'As well as savin' my neck you've done the State of Arizona a great service in wipin' out the Clancey gang. I'll clean up here and see to the paperwork, Major. You can see to whatever you were doin' before you decided to help to uphold United States' law.'

'We'll do that, Marshal,' the major said. He grinned at Alif. 'We are discovering that American horse traders have nothing to learn from their Afghan counterparts in trying to pull the wool over the eyes of prospective buyers.'

★ ★ ★

Marshal Bradwell would have another reason to thank Major Gaunt, though he would not know of it until the next morning long after the major and and his *compadres* had set off on their hunt for the killers of his sister.

On opening his office door, the marshal noticed an envelope addressed to him lying on the floor. Opening it, he found it contained two letters, one a legally worded document signed by the major. The other was a normal letter.

Dear Marshal, the letter began.

The enclosed document is to be posted to Mr S Carmody, the manager of the First National Bank, St Louis, Missouri. In the fullness of time the sum of money mentioned will be forwarded to you at a bank of your choice. Take it as payment for the future care and upkeep of my sister's grave. It should allow you to buy stock for that horse ranch you desire to own. It would be easier on your family's nerves than you wearing a marshal's badge.

Kindest regards to you and your family,

Major Philip Gaunt

PS Looking at our task realistically, there is a strong likelihood that we could both be killed. If it is possible I would appreciate it if our bodies could be recovered and given a decent burial. I would like to be buried alongside my sister. Alif, being of the Muslim faith, would not rest comfortably next to what he would call, infidels. Any spot on the open plain, as long as he is buried facing the east, would be fine.'

The marshal was lost for words. In a sort of a daze he walked on to the porch, still holding the letters. He gazed thoughtfully along the western trail leading out of town. 'Major,' he said, 'I wish you all the luck in the world, and then some, in your venture. But if the worst comes to the worst I'll honour your wish, no matter how long it takes and even if it means crossing into old Mexico.' He turned and walked back into his office to see to posting the letter to St Louis.

4

They were trailing south, in the direction of where his sister's killers must have their base, or so the major fervently hoped.

When their small column rode out of Bitter Water Creek, the major had asked Buckskin to take him to where the ambush had taken place. There he had spent several minutes deep in his own private thoughts as he contemplated the death scene. Then he pulled his mount's head round and rode back the several yards to Alif and Buckskin.

His face as unyielding as the ground they were riding across, he looked at Buckskin. 'Was, was she . . . ?' His voice broke.

'No, Major,' replied Buckskin, sombre-voiced. 'She was killed outright, as were all the passengers on the stage.' On the marshal's advice he kept silent about having to bury the girl to protect her body.

The major gave his guide an appraising glance. He seemed to be measuring up to his standards. He smelt and looked cleaner and had even gone to the trouble to cut short his wild mane of hair. And for all the drinking Mr Carlson had said he had done, he seemed reasonably alert for the hazards ahead of them.

'I haven't yet thanked you for your Christian act of taking my sister's body into Bitter Water Creek, Mr Carlson,' he said. The major's face softened slightly. 'But I had a lot on my mind back there in that town.'

Buckskin's spark of pride flared higher, the major still called him Mr Carlson. Not Buckskin, not drunken asshole, or dirty stinking bum, but had addressed him as an equal. From now on in, 'Mr Carlson' thought it would be a battle between his newly discovered pride and his craving for what the preachers called, the 'demon drink'.

The major's nerves, highly tuned to unseen signs of danger after years of active service on the North-West Frontier, began suddenly to twitch painfully. He shot a glance at Alif to see if he confirmed his fears. The slight tensing of the big Afridi's face proved to him that he hadn't lost any of his self-preservation skills.

Alif turned and faced him, eyes glinting. '*Chapoa*, Major *sahib*?' he growled.

Philip, looking about him for the danger he could not yet see, nodded in agreement. 'I couldn't pick a more suitable spot to set up an ambush, Alif,' he said, and unclipped the flap of his pistol holster.

Buckskin was having the same disturbing feelings. What he had left of his guts was telling him there were Apache close by. But yet again his unease could be caused by his lack of liquor intake. It must be at least twelve hours since his last slug of whiskey. He hoped so. Though the major and his cold-eyed, brown-skinned partner had proved in Bitter Water Creek that they were men of quick decisions and firm, deadly actions, and if luck came their way, could put paid to the killers they were trying to hunt down, if they ran into Geronimo and his band of white-eye slayers then by hell they were odds they could not face, and talk about it later.

Buckskin made a hasty but solid promise that he would shoot himself dead rather than suffer the slow painful death Geronimo would take a delight in inflicting on the three of them. Just then he noticed that the odds against them had stretched even further; the big Alif had disappeared. The bastard must have smelt trouble and cut and run for it. He did some more cursing. Before he got over that shock his fears were frighteningly realized.

Not twenty feet ahead of him five mounted Apache shot out of an arroyo as if sent from hell by Old Nick himself. And the squat-built, ugly-faced son-of-a-bitch up on the ragged-looking pinto was the number one devil himself, Geronimo. Heart pounding fit to burst he heard the major say, 'I take it that those ruffians blocking our way, Mr Carlson, are a bunch of those fierce Apache you told me about.'

'You're durn right, Major,' he managed to croak from a fear-dried throat. 'And that ruffian you're eyeballin' is the most bloodthirsty Apache in the whole South-West. Why, half the US Cavalry are chasin' their own asses tryin' to rope him in. We're as good as dead!' came out as a choking sob.

The major wasn't a man to be intimidated by reputations however fearful they may be. He had fought against men whose deeds of devilry would break the hearts of every saint in Heaven. He kneed his horse close up to the Apache chief.

'Chief Geronimo,' he began. 'I hope you can understand what I am saying. I have no quarrel with your people, I am

60

not an American. I come from a country far, far away and I am here on your land only to seek out the men, not of your people, Chief, who killed my only sister. Once I have done that I will leave this land and go back to my own people.'

Geronimo's eyebrows twitched in surprise and puzzlement on his cruel mask of a face. Only one other white-eye had been so bold to have come this close to him without a gun in his hand, the bluecoat General Crook, an *hombre* he favoured as an *amigo*. The white-eye who wasn't a gringo had the same direct-eyed gaze. He couldn't recognize the uniform he wore but he sat up on his horse as straight-backed as any pony soldier. And he had the strong face of a man used to giving out orders. No less a chief than he was.

Philip caught a glimpse of the uncertainty in the black, shoe-button eyes and heard the ominous restlessness of the other Apache as they waited, impatiently, for their chief to give the order to kill. Though the confrontation he was facing still ran along a knife's edge he had won enough time to show Geronimo his hand, or to be exact, Alif's hands, the hands that would be aiming the rifle on the Apache chief behind some rocks at the foot of the cliffs.

No soldier serving on the North-West Frontier would have a long life if he didn't have the ability to think several moves ahead when he just sensed possible danger, and act on them without orders from his superiors. Alif acted as he had thought fit. Philip smiled at Geronimo.

'I know you have been tracking us for quite a while, Chief,' he said. 'And right now you are racking your brains wondering where the third member of our party is. Well, I will put your mind at rest, he's behind some rock or other aiming his rifle at you.' The major's face steeled over. 'So, if it is in your mind to kill us, you will also die. Then your enemies will do a victory dance over your grave and you will have failed to free your people from the hated white-eyes. And I will die dishonoured for not avenging my sister's death.' To hone Geronimo's mind on the dilemma he was facing, the major yelled out an order in Pushtu.

The Snider's discharge resounded deafeningly from the rocks, and the banshee wail of its heavy slug could be clearly heard as it passed over the Apaches' heads, tearing off a branch of a branch of a wizened tree twenty feet beyond them. They clung tightly to their high-kicking spooked mounts, alarmed and angry-faced, crying out what the major believed were Apache curse words.

Buckskin closed his eyes and sweated blood. It was too late for any prayers. The Grim Reaper was about to tap him on the shoulder. Geronimo didn't like to be made a fool of, especially right in front of his wild boys. To his surprise, he saw Geronimo raise a calming hand and look at the major then spoke to him in Apache. Buckskin gave a real smile and believed there were such things as miracles.

'The gist of what the old butcher's spoutin', Major,' he cried out, 'is that he admires a man with balls, even a hated white-eye. He knows that shot coulduv killed him if you had so wished it. He reckons he owes you a favour. That favour is he has no quarrel with you and wishes you luck in catchin' your sister's killers.'

A relieved Philip sank back in his saddle then, leaning over, he reached across and put out his hand. Without hesitation, Geronimo gripped it in a firm handshake. Philip was sure he saw a glint of humour on the knife-like creased face.

'The man who fired that shot, Chief,' he said, 'is my comrade, a warrior of a tribe in a far country as fierce and as brave as the Apache.' He raised his voice, yelling out in English, 'Alif, you can come on down! We are in no danger!'

Alif came into view, holding the Snider loosely in his right hand. The major gave a grunt of pride and satisfaction. The six-foot Afridi with his puggaree, long woollen shirt, baggy pants, sun glinting off the brass shell cases of the Snider reloads in the bandoleer slung across his chest, and the big knife stuck in his belt, was a fearsome sight to behold, even by seasoned warriors.

The major heard the 'seasoned' warriors' hisses of surprise and even Geronimo's stoic look slipped somewhat. Alif, whiskers bristling, face set in the bold lines of some forgotten Roman caesar's death mask, was a man anyone would be foolish to cross. Geronimo, the major hoped, would recognize a kindred spirit, a fellow warrior from a warrior race and not be put out at being outwitted.

'This is Alif Khan, Chief Geronimo,' Philip said, with some ceremony. 'A great slayer of the enemies of my people.'

For a moment or two Alif and Geronimo, unblinking-eyed, gazed at each other, acknowledging each other as equals. Geronimo broke the the silence by speaking in Apache, still eye-balling Alif.

'The chief says he would like a closer look at that cannon your pard's totin', Major,' Buckskin said. 'He ain't seen one so fancy-lookin' before. The bang it makes and the lump of lead it throws reminds me of the .50 calibre Sharps buffalo gun. What the Injuns call the rifle that fires in the mornin' and kills what it hits in the afternoon.'

Without waiting for orders from the major, Alif handed up the Snider to Geronimo. He knew that the chief was a man of honour. Geronimo had talked peace with the Major *sahib* and that would be so.

Geronimo handled the rifle with the dexterity of the expert rifleman he was, his face visibly showing his admiration of its balance and its ornate, brass-studded stock. Then, after a few favourable comments on the rifle to his warband, he handed it back to Alif with a smile and a curt, '*Bueno!*'

Alif felt a feeling of natural pride. He hadn't understood what the chief had said about his rifle but he had seen that Geronimo had been impressed with it. Though it had started its life as a Snider, it was really his gun. He had originally taken it from a Mashud whose throat he had slit during a night attack on a hill fort. Then, spending days over a forge fire, he had lengthened and strengthened the barrel, fancy-working the stock, until he had a weapon to his satisfaction. A rifle a man would willingly give his wives to own.

Alif slung the rifle over his left shoulder then drew out his big Kabuli knife. Apache eyes widened at the sight of the long, glistening, blue-tinged blade, comparing it with their dull metal trade knives. It even dwarfed Geronimo's broad-bladed Bowie. Alif saw the look of envy in Geronimo's eyes. He held the knife before him in both hands.

'I will give it to you, Chief,' he said in English. 'As a gift from one warrior to another as is the custom among my people when we make peace. It was made by a man skilled in working iron.' Alif favoured Geronimo with a tight-lipped smile. 'It has drawn much blood.'

Geronimo managed to hang on to his dignity as a great war chief not to make a grab for the knife with both hands. His widely grinning braves watched him take hold of the offered knife and begin slashing at the air about him to get the feel of the big blade, uttering grunts of satisfaction as he did so.

'*Shabash*, good, you cunning devil, Alif,' muttered an equally pleased Philip. If you weren't such a fearsome-visaged man you would make an excellent diplomat, he thought. You have made sure the chief will stand by his *Pakhtunwali* by giving him the knife. The pair of them were out here in an unknown land with only an ex-drunk as an ally. Making friends with a potential enemy could only be to their ultimate advantage.

Geronimo spoke again, this time in halting English and directly at Philip.

'It is right that chiefs should exchange gifts of friendship.' Geronimo grinned slightly. 'But as you see we travel for war. Though I will honour this stone-faced warrior's gift by offering you the friendship of not only the warriors I have with me but the whole of my warband. You can go and seek out your sister's killers freely, no Apache will hinder you. Geronimo's word is law among my people, the Mimbreño.'

Before Philip could thank Geronimo for the outcome he had hoped for, the Apaches, with a slight flurry of hoof-raised dust, had vanished as abruptly as they had appeared.

Buckskin didn't know whether to laugh or cry at finding himself still alive. He hadn't felt so much happiness at one time in his life before even to raise a smile. He began to cry, the tears ran unashamedly down his grey, grizzled cheeks. He wouldn't have given a hoot if he'd pissed his pants. He had eye-balled the most feared man in the territory and was still alive, and now his goddamned *amigo*, the English major and his brown-skinned pard, were genuine, walk-the-line-with *hombres*. He couldn't be safer if he was riding with a whole troop of cavalry.

'Major,' he said, 'we've just taken a stroll into Daniel's den, said howdee to the lions and came out smilin'. Though it'll take me some time to stop shakin'.'

Philip turned in his saddle and grinned at him. 'Mr Carlson,' he said, 'you may not believe it, but I wasn't sitting comfortable in my saddle either. Men who have no conception of fear such as Alif and Geronimo are very rare indeed.'

Alif walked back across to the rocks, this time to return with his horse. Buckskin saw that he had another knife in his belt. 'Has the big fella got a collection of those pig-stickers, Major?' he asked.

'Just the two,' the major replied. 'Alif would rather have died than give up his only knife. They are sort of family pieces so to speak, handed down from father to son.' Then reflecting for a few seconds, he said, 'In fact, when Alif drew his knife I thought he intended to disembowel Geronimo.' He grinned again at Buckskin. 'Then, by George, those lions would have been well and truly aroused.'

Buckskin swallowed hard, his good humour waning as he fought off an urgent need to evacuate his bowels. He knew the big man was a killing man, a Geronimo, from wherever he hailed, but he was just getting the measure of the quietspoken English major. He had a hardness an enemy wouldn't discover until it was too late to do anything about but die. And he had to keep up with the pair of hellions if he had any pride as a Westerner left, and a tight hold of his bowels.

'An hour's ride from here, Major,' he said, 'is a water-hole. The next water we'll see will be below the border in old Mexico. I opine we should make camp there for the night. And it would wise to hit the trail early to cover some territory before the sun peaks. It's as hot as hell down there this time of the year.' Buckskin grinned. 'I know that the heat don't worry you and Mr Alif none, but it's hard on the horses and we'll not have any water to spare.'

'You are the guide, Mr Carlson,' the major replied. 'I will abide by your decision.'

'One other thing, Major,' Buckskin said. 'We'll have to travel less openly. As I told you I don't know where those murderin' assholes hole-up, but there's Mex villages below the border, they could be in any of them. And they'll not be the only bunch of *bandidos* roamin' hereabouts. Though not bein' a military man, I figure we ought not to attract attention from those cut-throats by ridin' as though we're on some county turnpike.'

The major didn't tell Buckskin that he had already taken into account the necessity of remaining unseen to any potential enemy ahead of them. He was pleased that Mr Carlson, the drunk Alif had literally dragged out of a saloon and sobered up, was beginning to show spirit and think straight and act like the guide he was supposed to be.

'Good thinking, Mr Carlson,' he said. 'I'll send Alif forward on foot. It's the type of country he was raised in. He will be able to move with some speed and ought to give us advance warning of any danger coming our way. Now lead us to that water you spoke of, Mr Carlson.'

5

'Your *amigo*, Geronimo, Major,' Buckskin said, 'ain't that far ahead of us, see?' He pointed to his left. The major and Alif saw the smoke rising in a straight dark pillar in the middle distance.

'That's the red hellion's callin'-card,' continued Buckskin. 'Some poor Mex sodbuster and his family will be lying butchered in the burnin' ruins of their shack.'

The major and Alif exchanged knowing glances. They had often witnessed such scenes of destruction and death along their frontier; they were travelling across familiar ground.

'We're south of the border now, Major,' Buckskin began again. 'Ridin' across Don Carlo Argumedo's land. His piece of dirt stretches as far as you can see, and beyond, south-east and west of us. Another hour or so we oughta be raisin' his fine hacienda.' He grinned at the major. 'M'be it ain't as big and as grand-lookin' as some of your English castles, but it ain't to be sneezed at. It was built by one of the first Spanish settlers who planted their roots here more than eighty years ago. He'll oblige us by lettin' us water our stock at one of his wells.'

★   ★   ★

'*Patron*,' said Zolando. 'There's riders coming in from the border.'

'I see them,' Don Carlo replied to his hacienda straw boss. 'It seems only a small party so it is not a patrol of gringo Texas Rangers in pursuit of some of our *bandidos*,' he added.

'They could be gringo gold-seekers.'

'Don't the loco gringos know that there is only death for small bands of riders here in Sonora, Zolando?' Geronimo and his war bands would see to that he thought. He had sent out a strong, well-armed party of *vaqueros* to one of his peons' homes when one of the hacienda guards reported seeing smoke in the direction of the house. They would be too late to be of any help to his tenant and his family. They were always too late to do anything but bury the dead. Geronimo struck as swiftly and deadly as a snake, then like the snake disappeared among the rocks.

* * *

'The small man wearing the white hat, Major, is Don Carlo Argumedo himself,' Buckskin said. 'He ain't an impressive figure of a man to look at, but he holds in his hands the lives of every man, woman and child on his land. The hatchet-faced *hombre* is Zolando, the man who sees that the don's orders are carried out. He's the bossman of over thirty *vaqueros* and several thousand head of cattle. A chore not likely to put a smile on a fella's face.'

The major saw that the don was a great deal older than he was as he rode nearer to the two horsemen. He had the aquiline face of a Spanish grandee and the authoritative look of a man who had been born to command, like his own family had. Though apart from the family estate in England left to him from another branch of the family, all the land the Gaunts had acquired through their army service in India was a grave dug out of sandy soil at the foot of some barren mountain range. Yet the major would rather have it that way than be responsible for the well-being of all the lives on the don's vast holdings.

The don was making his own assessment of the three strangers riding across his land. The leading rider, though he was a white man, didn't ride like a gringo. He took a longer, puzzled look at the big, bearded man who was neither Mexican nor Apache. The don, no mean judge of men, thought he was an *hombre* who would be able to hold his own against any man, of any race. The third member of the party didn't need any assessing, he would be the straight-backed rider's guide.

Guide for what, the don thought? A hunting trip? The only hunting going on in Sonora was being done by Geronimo and his war bands and their prey were Mexicans, men, women and children.

Zolando, paid to be constantly on the look-out for any trouble against his *patron*'s property and stock, and deal with it pronto, was also casting an appraising look at the bearded rider. And came up with the same opinion of the rider as the don. If roused, Zolando opined, the big man could be real trouble. He fixed a hard-eyed, watchful stare on him.

The major smiled and touched the brim of his hat in a greeting salute. 'Good day, Don Argumedo, I'm Major Gaunt, a visitor to your country. Forgive us for trespassing on your land, but our water supplies are running low. I am hoping you will be kind enough to allow us to water our animals at your well.'

The don's eyes widened in surprise. An Ingles? If the Englishman had not stated he was a major he would have known by his carriage and direct-eyed manner of speaking that he was a man of some consequence, a *caballerro* no less.

'You are welcome at the Hacienda La Carendo, Major Gaunt,' he said. 'You are the first Englishman I have met.' He smiled. 'And the likes of your bearded *compañero* I surely haven't seen before. He has even impressed Señor Zolando, the hacienda *jefe*.'

The major smiled back at him. 'That is Alif Khan, Don Argumedo. A great friend, in peace and war. He has left his homeland halfway around the world to serve with me. And is fiercer than he looks when roused.'

The don laughed. 'We are used to *broncos* in Mexico, Major. Take our guests to water their stock, Zolando, and ask the cook to prepare a hot meal for them. Though I would deem it a favour, Major, if you would dine with me and my wife. She will be most interested to hear you tell her about the female fashions in London.'

The burning urge to keep on the trail of his sister's killers, however futile it could turn out to be in the end, burnt painfully like a fire inside the major. 'You do me a great honour Don Argumedo,' he replied, 'but I will have to turn down your kind invitation. I do not wish to be churlish but it is imperative I continue my journey south while there are still several hours of daylight left.' He then told the don the reason why he was in Mexico.

The don listened impassively. He wanted to tell the Ingles major that it was a suicide mission he was embarked on, for the three of them. Though, he thought, if his wife had suffered the same terrible fate he would have hunted down the killers, with his small army of *vaqueros* riding alongside him. So, instead, he said, 'It is a dangerous undertaking, Major; there are many *bandidos*, and the Apache, Geronimo.' He shrugged. 'You and your *compadres* face fearful odds.'

The major smiled slightly. 'I have already met Geronimo, Don Argumedo,' he said. 'And he assures me of his friendship, and neither he, nor any of his warriors, will hinder me in my search for the killers.'

'*Madre de Dios!*' the don gasped, his face losing its stoic, aristocratic look. 'You have met Geronimo?' Was the Ingles lying? Yet he didn't think that an Ingles *caballero* would lie to his face. 'Not many *hombres* have gazed at that red devil's face and lived, Major.'

'Mr Carlson, my guide, has made that same observation, Don Argumedo.' replied Philip. 'That means we only have the *bandidos* to worry about. The gang I'm hunting comprises of five men, three Mexican and two Americans. One of the Mexicans is their leader.'

Only the *bandidos* to worry about. The don mentally shook his head disparagingly. Were the Ingles a race of madmen? Yet the major's cool, steady gaze didn't show any wild gleam of insanity. For a man who could win Geronimo's friendship in so short a time, it would be logical to think that several dozen Mexican *bandidos* should not present him with too much of a problem. After all, his ancestors, the *Conquistadores*, had taken on bigger odds and won through.

'I do not know of the *bandidos* you mention,' he said. 'But there is a village thirty miles south of here which is often frequented by *bandidos* who, when they have the urge for the pleasures of a woman, come down from their hideouts in the mountains to sate their lust on the cantina girls. Maybe you could seek intelligence there regarding the men you seek.'

The don stern-eyed Philip. 'Though you will have to be discreet in your enquiries. You will be gringos to the villagers, gringos with much to steal, and they do not hold any friendship for men who come from north of the Rio Bravo. You will have to look on them with distrust, that they could be in league with the *bandidos*.' The don paused for a moment or two. Then he continued, 'Also there are the Rurales and Federales, Mexican Army and law-enforcing patrols. They will not take kindly to seeing gringos this far south of the border. They will be suspicious and could treat you roughly before you can explain your reason for being in Mexico. If they are Rurales, they could shoot you and take your horses and supplies. Many of them are no better than the *bandidos* they are supposed to be hunting. So, before you ride out, I will give you a paper signed by me for you to show to any Mexican officer, stating that you and your *compadres* are friends of Don Carlo

Argumedo and are to be treated with respect and courtesy. I do not wish you, Major Gaunt, to think that only a bloodthirsty savage can offer you the hand of friendship in Mexico.'

'It has been a pleasure to have made your acquaintance, sir,' Philip said. 'And if things go well for me I'll ride back this way and have that meal with your family, if the offer is still open.' He grinned. 'Though it is an engagement I would only pencil in your diary.'

'*Bueno*,' replied the don. 'A place at my table will always be waiting for you, Major.' He leaned across his saddle and took the major's hand in a firm grip. 'And I hope you will taste the sweetness of revenge.'

The major gave the don a first-class military salute, then turning his horse, kneed it into a gentle trot in the direction the don had indicated.

The don watched him thinking that the Ingles major would need the friendship of the Good Lord himself if

he was to see him sitting at his table in
the big hall of the hacienda.

★ ★ ★

The three hunters were once again
riding south, to the village that had
links with *bandidos*. Zolando had
named it, San Jerome, and, like the
don, had warned them to be always on
their guard if they wanted to stay alive.

They were riding in silence, deep in
their own thoughts. The major trying
not think too much of the enormity of
his task to find the five bandits who had
raided the stage in a land that seemed
full of bandits.

Alif unconsciously fingered the
handle of his big knife. By Allah, he
thought, he could smell blood-letting.
Maybe not the blood of the cowardly
dogs they were hunting, but the major
sahib's and his own enemies neverthe-
less.

Buckskin was wrestling with his
new-found pride. He had signed on as

guide and to identify the killers, if ever they got within looking distance of the sons-of-bitches. Once he did that, and the guns came out, he had the major's permission to cut and run for it. What was rubbing him raw was the way big Alif still looked down his nose at him. The big bastard didn't think he had the backbone to stand up alongside him and the major. And that irked Buck-skin. While he admitted he'd never had the cold-blooded courage of the big heathen and the major, since giving up the bottle he was regaining some of the grit that had carried him through the War. Buckskin clenched his teeth and nudged his horse alongside the major's.

'I ain't wishin to speak outa turn, Major,' he said, 'like tellin' you what your next moves should be, but we oughta take serious the don and his straw boss's warnin' about the *bandido* situation in San Jerome.'

'Mr Carlson,' the major replied, 'all our lives are at stake in this hunt. You have every right to state your opinions on how we should proceed. Indeed I would welcome them.' He smiled thinly at Buckskin. 'I have very few of my own. Other than trying to capture some *bandido* to question him regarding the men we are seeking, in the very big hope he can give us some information concerning them. And that, Mr Carlson, as you would put it, ain't no plan at all.'

'Well, Major,' Buckskin said, his confidence growing, 'I figure that those buildin's showin' up on the skyline is San Jerome. For the three of us to ride in there bold as you please is temptin' our luck more than somewhat bein' that the place could be full of *bandidos*.'

'I take your point, Mr Carlson,' the major said. 'Alif and I don't actually blend into the background, so to speak. What do you suggest?'

'I'll go in on my own,' replied Buckskin. 'One old, ragged-assed gringo drifter shouldn't attract much attention. If there ain't no *bandidos* hangin' around the cantina, I could m'be play up to one of the girls, ask her when some of the owlhoots are due in town.' He grinned. 'We could get your *bandido* to question, Major.'

'That is as good a plan as any, Mr Carlson,' Philip said. 'But remember, be discreet in your enquiries. We have to take it that the villagers, or at least some of them, are in league with gangs until we can prove otherwise. Now I suggest we make camp here; it will be dark soon and I don't want to risk running into trouble in the dark on land we don't know. We will put your plan into action in daylight, Mr Carlson.'

6

A shivery, bleary-eyed Buckskin greeted the new day with a silent cheer. A cold camp without a gutful of whiskey to warm him up and dull his senses was pure hell, a ball-freezing hell. He would be glad to get on the move again, even if it meant he was riding into a nest of cut-throat greaser *bandidos*.

He mounted his mule for the short ride into San Jerome. The mule had been doing service as one of the pack animals, but, as he explained to the major, a mule was more in keeping with his role as a drifter than riding into the village sitting up on a fine horse.

'There's more men been killed over the possession of a horse,' he said, 'than there have been in disputes over women.' He grinned at Alif. 'I figure it's the same in the territory you hail from, pard.'

Alif gave Buckskin his first friendly grin. The old man was acting and thinking like a fighting warrior.

Buckskin's spirits rose. His cold, cramped limbs eased. At last the big savage was on his way to accepting him as a partner. He was looking forward to riding into San Jerome, *bandido* occupied or not. By thunder, he thought, he was the only gringo in the party, it was up to him to show his pards what calibre of men fought for old Abe Lincoln.

'Take care, Mr Carlson,' the major said. 'And I don't wish for us to stay here longer than we have to. We will rendezvous with you at those trees to the left of the village at noon. If you have no news in our favour that I can act upon, we move on. We can't stay hidden from the peons this close to their village for too long. We are short in numbers, Mr Carlson; fair game for any gang of outlaws, so it is to our great advantage to keep our presence hereabouts a secret.' He smiled up at

Buckskin. 'Try your damnedest to bring me some good news.'

'I'll do my best, Major,' Buckskin replied. 'See you at the trees then.' He jerked at the reins and the mule broke into a heavy-footed lumbering trot.

★   ★   ★

Through his army glasses, the major watched the distant figure of Mr Carlson dismount outside one of the larger buildings in the village, the cantina, he surmised. He nodded at Alif. 'Right, Alif, off you go and watch over our friend. If he lands in trouble I know you will deal with it swiftly. But if possible I would prefer it to be done silently. As I said, we have to move across this land as noislessly as ghosts so as not to alert any potential enemies.'

Alif favoured his major with a fearsome all-toothed smile. He slung a Winchester across his shoulder, then, drawing his knife, slipped out of the hollow in which they had made camp, on foot.

A slow smile crossed the major's face. He had been Alif's CO for almost twelve years, yet the big ox of a man still surprised him as to how quickly he could use the lie of the ground to his advantage, even ground he had not stepped a foot on before. Alif hadn't gone four or five yards and he had already lost sight of him.

Buckskin took several glances about him. This early in the day San Jerome seemed to be a village of the dead. He reckoned that even when every peon and their families were up and about doing their chores the village wouldn't have a rip-roaring look about it. Though early or not, at least one Mexican had dragged himself out of his bed, the cantina door was open.

Buckskin felt a tightness in his throat. He had more fretting away inside him than the possibility of eyeballing some Mexican bad-asses. The 'demon drink' was only a few steps behind him. He was about to get the smell of strong liquor for the first time since he had been forcibly sobered up. Cursing at his weakness he straightened his shoulders. He'd be damned if he was going to let the major or Alif down, two men who were treating him as an equal partner. Maybe, he thought, grinning, the cantina sold strong soda pop.

By the flickering flames of two storm lanterns pegged on the rear wall of the cantina, Buckskin saw that the bar was empty. He had also seen cleaner and more solidly built hogpens. He grunted. He was thinking like a Bible-thumper. He had been laid out drunk as a skunk in suchlike dumps. He heard voices out back and walked across to the rear door which, like the front door, was wide open.

On stepping outside, Buckskin discovered there were more people awake in San Jerome than the cantina owner. The first people to make their presence known to him were two hard-faced, double-armed Mexicans standing alongside a stagecoach. They swung round, covering him with their rifles.

Buckskin's hands grabbed at air high above his head.

'Friend, *amigos*!' he cried out. 'I ain't any trouble! I'm just a gringo driftin' through!'

The two men lowered their rifles, slowly, but not their guard. Both of them still favoured him with wary-eyed suspicious looks. Just as slowly, Buckskin lowered his arms and began to breathe again, and had the chance to take in the whole scene at the rear of the cantina.

A young girl, with bloodstains on her blouse, was sitting on a packing trunk having the wound on her right shoulder tended to by an elderly female dressed in black. Judging by the pale, pain-racked face, Buckskin thought it was a bad wound. The coach door had some sort of a bird, gold in colour, emblazoned on its door so he reckoned the girl was an important Mexican's daughter.

The Mexican wearing a dirty white apron standing next to the old lady and holding a dish must be the cantina owner.

'More water, pronto!' Buckskin heard the elderly woman say, then saw her lift up her ankle-length skirt and begin to tear strips off a white undergarment to use as a bandage.

The cantina owner shot Buckskin a drop-dead look as he brushed past him. Buckskin followed him through and out of the cantina and caught up with him as he was lowering the bucket down into the well.

He had been sent into the village to seek information, finding out who had shot the girl could be of some importance to the major.

'How came the young *señorita* by her wound, *amigo*?' he asked.

'*Bandidos*, gringo,' he snarled. 'She is Señorita Ortero, niece of the Don Argumedo.' He gave Buckskin a baleful-eyed look. 'You are lucky her escort did not shoot you. Two of the *bandidos* were gringo dogs!'

'Jesus H. Christ!' gasped Buckskin. The major's hunt for his sister's killers wasn't going to be a long shot after all. And it was news he would want to hear straight away, from the men who had first-hand knowledge of the *bandidos*.

He hurried back through the cantina and again had to face the nervous jerking of two rifles targeting him. Buckskin could sympathize with the escorts' feelings. They had lost a lot of their pride in allowing their charge to come to harm. The don, when he heard of his niece being wounded, would have their balls.

'My pard,' he said, walking close up to the two escorts, 'is an English army major and he's camped just outside the village. Among the supplies we're carryin' is a medicine chest. It's up to you *hombres* to tell me to bring him on in. I ain't a doc but by the look of it the *señorita*'s wound needs more attention that just cleanin' it out with well water.'

José Silba, the senior escort, was between a rock and a hard place. As well as the *señorita* being wounded he had lost three of his men in the ambush. Indeed, if Romero hadn't handled the coach with great skill, squeezing it past the barricade of stones the *bandidos* had laid across the trail, then keeping it upright in the wild ride across country, the whole party would have been killed. The *bandidos*, he reasoned, would not pursue them to the village. They had been expecting an easy killing from an ambuscade, not a prolonged gunfight with expert riflemen. But he could be wrong. And if he was, he could expect no help from the unarmed, *pacifico* villagers.

The dilemma he was in was that the *señorita* was in no fit state to make the rough stage ride to the safety of Don Argumedo's hacienda. If he sent Romero, his *compadre*, to ride to the hacienda for help he would be left here on his own with two women to protect. And the *bandidos*, if they showed up, would achieve what they failed to do on the trail. And in the time he was waiting for Romero to return with aid, the Señorita Ortero would be suffering great pain. The old gringo was right, she needed proper medicine.

He hawk-eyed the old man. Was he a member of a gang of Yankee *bandidos*, and his offer of help a ploy for him and Romero to drop their guard? The old man didn't have the cut of a *mal hombre*. And he spoke of his *compadre* being an English army major, a *caballero*, and who would do no harm to them. Or so he had to believe.

'You bring that officer here, *gringo*,' he said at last, still unfriendly, scowling at Buckskin as he spoke.

Buckskin grinned. Things were working out for the major real good. The two parties could help each other. The Mexicans could give them a hot trail to the men they were hunting. He hoped the major's medical skills were good enough to ease the girl's pain and please the Indian-faced Mexican.

'I'll go and signal him to come on in, *amigo*,' he said, praying that the major would show up first. The Mexican escorts catching sight of Alif on his own, toting his big rifle, the slaughter-house knife and festooned with reloads would think that a one man *bandido* gang was descending on them. And act accordingly.

An anxious waiting major saw his guide come out of the cantina and begin waving his hat. His face bright-ened and eased his lip chewing. Mr Carlson must have some important news for him. He lowered his glasses and got to his feet.

★ ★ ★

'The old fart has come back out of the cantina,' Hank Norris said. 'All who's up and about in this dog-dirt dump is at that stage. As I said when we first saw the stage haul in here, that young lady who's been gunshot must have a rich pa. I reckon right now it's time we strolled in on 'em and persuaded the gal to open up her cases and hand over her trinkets and any hard cash she's got stowed away.'

Josh gave his partner a sour-faced look. 'And that's all we'll take,' he growled. 'What we can cram into our saddle-bags. We ain't drivin' that stage team to the border, we get to hell out of it fast. That Rurale patrol we bumped into could swing by this way at any time and my horse ain't in no fit state to be ass-kicked all the way to the Rio Grande.'

'That's OK by me, Josh,' replied Hank. 'I've had my bellyful of old Mexico as well. I'm willin' to take my chance dodgin' the Texas law boys.'

With Texas being too hot for men, who earned their wherewithal by a drawn and cocked gun, or the point of a knife at a throat, they had crossed the border hoping to find some rich Mexican don to rob. Much to Hank's disappointment they hadn't found any easy pickings in Sonora. Just piss poor sodbusters, dried-up women and rotgut liquor an Indian would turn up his nose at.

Then they really hit bad luck. A Rurale patrol jumped them. The greaser sons-of-bitches, Hank thought angrily, hadn't stopped to ask them their business in Mexico, all polite like. The bunch of them had just come fire-balling in on them blazing away with their carbines. Hank shuddered. He could still hear those shells whistling by his ears. Though Josh would agree that luck was now in their favour. Easy-pickings time was here. He grinned at Josh as they closed in on the stage, rifles held loosely across their chests.

Alif, face a grim mask, knife drawn, dogged the pair in a knee-and-elbow crawl. He had smelt tobacco smoke when he had first gone to ground to keep an eye on his major's guide as he talked to the men at the coach. Following in the direction of the smell, he had come across two men squatting in a dip in the ground. They, he noticed, were also interested in the coach. The old guide was in no danger, so he concentrated all his attention on the two men, who had the shifty-eyed faces of Afghan *badmash*.

Hank and Josh came round either side of the stage, rifles now held steady, and aimed with fingers on the triggers, to catch everyone there off guard.

'If either of you greasers try to bring your guns into play that purty young *señorita* will get another bullet in her,' a wide grinning Hank said. 'One that'll put her down for keeps. And my pard there will see that the *señora* goes the same way.' Hank fish-eyed Buckskin. 'This dispute is between us and these Mexes, so it ain't of your business, pilgrim. But if you feel you oughta poke your nose in, the same rule applies: pull out a gun and those ladies get dead.'

José cast a venomous glare at Hank though he indicated to Romero that he should drop his rifle and he did likewise. Buckskin drew out his pistol and threw it well away from him. He didn't want any blame to fall on him if the sons-of-bitches carried out their threats and killed the women.

Pablo, the cantina owner, muttered a shaky-voiced, '*Madre de Dios*,' and dropped the bowl he was holding, the water it held splashing all over his pants and sandals.

'We'll not bother you folks long,' Hank said, his confident, easy-takings grin showing again. 'We just want to take a peek into the *señorita*'s cases and take out what suits our purpose. You help the girl on to her feet, *señora*, so that fat, little greaser can open them. You go and check them out, Josh, I'll keep a bead on the girl. You plug the old woman if those two Mexes decide not to co-operate.'

Alif waited until Josh had moved ahead of Hank. He gave a satisfied smile. It gave him the chance to kill one man before the other realized he was on his own and only a second or two from death himself, giving him no time to carry out his threat to shoot the young girl and her chaperon. He got on to his knees and unslung his rifle and held it in his left hand. He drew his right hand back then brought it forward sharply in an overarm arc. The knife blade glinted chillingly in the sunlight as it hissed through the air.

Hank grunted with pain as he felt a thudding blow between his shoulder-blades that sent him stumbling forward a pace. Then came the sickening taste of thick blood welling up into his throat as the everlasting darkness of death numbed all his senses.

Josh heard Hank's rasping gasp and his natural reaction was to swing round to find out why. He had only the split second of time to see Hank falling face down to the ground, no time to register shocked surprise, before Alif's shot punched a fist-sized exit hole in the back of his head, The *señorita* screamed as he fell at her feet.

Alif growled several Pushtu curses. He had only meant to wound the man in his shoulder so that the major *sahib* could question him to find out if he could give them information on the men whom they were hunting. It was the first time he had fired the Winchester and he hadn't known it pulled to the left. He strode across to his first kill and, bending down, he yanked his knife out of the body, wiping it clean of blood on the dead man's clothes before slipping it back into his belt.

José and Romero reached down for their discarded rifles as the swift killer of the two gringo *bandidos*, a Yaqui-faced giant of a man dressed in a fashion no Yaqui or Apache, favoured, walked towards them.

'It's OK, *amigos*,' a beaming-faced Buckskin called out. 'It's Señor Alif, the major's man!' He waved for Alif to keep on coming in.

Major Gaunt on hearing the shot, let go of the lead ropes of the pack animals and kneed his mount into a gallop for the rear of the cantina, Alif's horse cantering alongside him. Mr Carlson had signalled for him to come into the village, what the hell had gone wrong, he wondered?

José and Romero still eyed Alif suspiciously but made no threatening moves towards him with their rifles. Alif glanced down at Josh's body, thinking briefly that if he had brought the Snider with him the major *sahib* would have had a prisoner to interrogate. Though, thinking again, the wound his big rifle made, the *badmash* would be in no fit state to talk for several days. He then caught sight of the wounded girl and his hard-cut face softened somewhat. Ignoring the men with the rifles he walked right up to the girl and stood there for a minute or two studying her wound.

'*Pani*, water!' he barked, towering over the cowering Pablo. Then indicated he wanted a glass of drinking water. The cantina owner shot a frightened what-do-I-do look at José.'

'Do as the old gringo's *compadre*

says,' José said, without any hesitation. He wasn't about to hinder any *hombre* who could ease Señorita Ortero's pain and prevent her wound going bad on her. And in spite of his fearsome look and expertise in killing with gun and knife, José was getting the feeling the big *hombre* could do that.

Pablo nodded. '*Sí!*' he croaked, and scurried away to get the water, glad to be out of the fierce *hombre*'s presence for a few minutes.

Señora Gutierez wasn't too happy to allow a strange *mal hombre* who looked as though he had Indian blood in him to lay his bloodstained hands on the *señorita*. Boldly she stood in front of Alif preventing him from getting any closer to her charge.

A shouted command in Spanish from José made her move aside, though showing her reluctance to do so by scowling fiercely at Alif.

Alif knelt down and gently took hold of Señorita Ortero's arm and took a good look at her wound. Fearful-eyed, the *señorita* tried to pull her hand from his.

'Do not be afraid, maiden, I will do you no harm,' he said, smiling.

While the smile wasn't as sweet as an altar boy's, Buckskin swore he never thought it possible for such a craggy-faced *hombre* to smile friendly at all. He turned as he heard the major come riding in and hurried over to explain the situation, as he dismounted. The major saw the two bodies and guessed what trouble there had been. Alif had cleared it up, quickly and permanently.

'The young girl, Major,' Buckskin said, 'is Don Argumedo's niece. She musta been shot by the same bunch of *bandidos* who killed your sister. So it looks like it ain't goin' to be such a wild gamble after all tryin' to hunt down those killers as you thought. When those Mexes tell you where those *bandidos* jumped their stage, that oughta give us a hot trail to follow. I thought it was only right to show our friendliness by offerin' to treat the girl's wound.'

'That is good news, Mr Carlson,' the major replied, his face showing the keenness and expectation of a man whose chosen mission wasn't a forlorn cause after all. He nodded in the direction of the two bodies. 'Were those two members of the gang we seek, Mr Carlson?' he asked.

Buckskin shook his head. 'Naw, Major,' he said. 'They're just a coupla Yankee bushwhackers thinkin' there was easy pickin's for them here.' He grinned. 'Mr Alif showed them otherwise. As you can see Alif's checkin' on the girl's wound so I reckon he'll need the medicine chest we're carrying.'

The major grinned. 'Mr Carlson,' he said 'Alif and his like have lived and soldiered in a land not unlike your Great Plains, lacking in doctors, let alone hospitals, to treat any wounds or illness that may befall them. Circumstances forced them to be their own doctors and surgeons, whatever. Alif is carrying enough powders and potions about his person, and taking into account his dexterity with his big knife, he could quite easily amputate a badly shot up limb with no more discomfort to the patient than he would suffer in a field-dressing station. Now I'll go and introduce myself to those two escorts and assure them that their female charge is in good hands.'

José and Romero automatically stiffened to attention as the old gringo's *jefe* came towards them. His clothes were as unfamiliar to them as the big knife-killing *hombre*'s were. Though they both recognized the straight-backed purposeful walk and the piercing, all-seeing look of a man who, like their *patron*, the don, told other men to do this and do that and it was done, pronto. José had no doubt that he was, as the gringo had told him, an army officer and a don in his own country.

'I am Major Gaunt, *señors*,' Philip said. 'To put your minds at rest the young *señorita* is in safe hands. I'm glad that we can be of some help.'

José was relieved enough to muster a ghost of a smile. They were strong enough now to beat off any possible attack by the *bandidos*. '*Muchas gracias, señor,*' he said. 'Now we have three extra guns I can send my *compadre*, Romero, to the Hacienda La Carendo for men to escort the coach to the hacienda. The *señorita* is the niece of my *patron*, Don Argumedo.'

'I know,' replied Philip, 'We have had the honour of meeting the don. We will see to her wound then I would like you to tell me about those *bandidos* who shot her. I believe they are the same band of killers I and my men are trying to hunt down.'

The major walked across to Alif leaving José wondering why a English don was risking his life and those of his men tracking down Mexican *bandidos*. He didn't seem loco.

On seeing the young girl's pain-drawn look, the major's face steeled over. Jennifer would have suffered such pain before she was killed. The *señorita* had been fortunate not to have suffered the same fate. Fiercely he renewed his vow to see the killers pay for their crimes.

'*Señorita*,' he said, softly, 'do not be afraid. Alif here may look fearsome but he is very good at treating wounds. He will soon have you back on the coach to continue your journey to the Hacienda La Carendo.' He smiled reassuringly at the still surly-faced chaperon then nodded to Alif. 'She's all yours, now, Alif, don't let the Rifles down.'

Alif drew out his knife and sliced off the whole of the ripped blouse sleeve on the girl's wounded arm. Taking the damp cloth from the *señora's* hands he dabbed at the wound until he could see the deep, jagged, bullet tear just below her shoulder. Reaching into a pocket of his goatskin coat, he pulled out two small leather satchels; he was ready to treat the vicious-looking wound.

An apprehensive Señorita Ortero

reached out with her good arm and gripped the major's hand. He squeezed it gently. The girl smiled at him wanly.

Romero had ridden out to the hacienda and Buckskin, after bringing in the pack animals, was standing guard with José and three early rising peons armed with the dead Yankee bandits' guns. Buckskin was standing close to Alif and his patient and nosy enough to ask the major how Alif was treating the wound.

'In that glass of water he got from the cantina owner,' the major said, 'he's put some powdered plant root and is giving it to the girl to drink. It's an opiate, a drug, and it will dull the pain she will feel when Alif dusts the open wound with the other powdered root. He has to clean the wound and prevent infection. Though it stings, it is a great deal less painful than cauterizing it with a hot bayonet or rod, and leaves no burn scar.'

The reinforcements from the Hacienda La Carendo, with Don Argumedo at their head, thundered in as Señora Gutierez was finishing tying the bandage on the *señorita*'s arm. Alif had stood back after he had treated the wound and allowed the elderly woman, impatient to do her part, to finish dressing the wound. Señora Gutierez had lost her hostility towards the big stranger when she saw that the wound had been expertly treated and the *señorita*'s face was not so pinched-looking. She was gracious enough to mutter, '*Bueno, muchas gracias.*'

An anxious-looking don swung down from his mount and rushed to his niece's side. His men, eight hard-faced, heavily armed *vaqueros*, also dismounted and quickly formed a defensive screen around the coach. Don Argumedo wasn't about to put his brother's daughter's life in danger again.

The *señora*, in her own language, told the don how the big *amigo*, servant of the gringo *caballero*, had treated the *señorita*'s wound as good as the hacienda's doctor could have done and that apart from the pain she should not suffer any ill-effects.

'It as Señora Guiterez says, Uncle,' Señorita Ortero said. 'I am fine; the wound has stopped bleeding and it does not pain so much.' She glanced up a Alif. 'Thank you, *señor*,' she said in English, sweet-smiling at him. 'I was frightened of you at first, but . . . '

Alif gave an acknowledging grunt and a flicker of a smile in response and put his packets of healing powders back into his pocket.

'And I thank you, *amigo*,' the don said. 'As in your land, I suppose, wounds can go bad if not treated quickly and properly. And thanks to you, Major, for guarding the coach by killing those two gringo *bandidos*.'

'Those thanks, Don Argumedo,' the major replied, 'should also go to Alif. Mr Carlson and I have only been bystanders at the happenings here.'

The don looked at the hawk-faced Alif. He thought that his *vaqueros* were proud, hard *hombres* but no *hombre*, Mexican, gringo or Indian could stand taller and prouder than the man who had treated his niece's wound. He could only guess at the inner quality and strength the Ingles major must have to command the loyalty of a company of such warriors.

'Romero has told me of the attack, Major,' he said grimly. 'Once I have escorted the *señorita* and the *señora* to the hacienda, ten of my *vaqueros* are yours to command in your hunt for the *bandidos*.'

'Though you have every right to join in the hunt, Don Argumedo,' the major said, 'I do not think it is wise tactics. They will easily see a large body of riders and go to ground until it is safe for them to take up their murderous ways again. If they only see three riders, the furthest thing from their minds will be that they are a threat to them. The way Alif and I are dressed will have them puzzled. Probably take me for a crazy gringo hunter. It could draw them out into the open and save us a lot of time trying to follow their trail.'

What the major said made sense, the don admitted, though as *jefe* over vast holdings of land and hundreds of peons he had to show that in the event of any attack on their lives or property, swift and bloody retribution would be taken against the men responsible.

The major sensed what was passing through the don's mind, that his refusal of help from him conflicted with the don's obligations to avenge the attack on his niece; like him, his pride and honour would demand it.

'You could still be of great help in the hunt for them, Don Argumedo,' he said. 'Send out your *vaqueros*, have them patrol, vigorously, north of Diablo Pass where your man José told me they were attacked. Seeing all that activity should restrict the territory they can safely move across.' The major smiled. 'And less land for us to try out our Judas goat tactics.'

The don thought of the Ingles

117

major's plan to act as a decoy, a normal ploy to draw out a mountain big cat that had been killing a village's livestock from its lair on to waiting rifles. Only this time, if he had judged the major correctly, it would be the unsuspecting goats being drawn into the jaws of the waiting lions. José coming up to him to tell him that his niece and the *señora* were settled comfortably in the coach and they were ready to move out, made up his mind.

'I will do as you suggest, Major,' he said. 'Once the *señorita* and the *señora* are safe at the hacienda, José will head a party of *vaqueros* and they will watch all trails leading north from the pass, though that will still leave a lot of land for you to search. So if you need any help you have only to ask for it, *comprende?*'

The don shook the major's hand and, wishing him God's favour, mounted his horse and gave the command to move out.

The three *compañeros* watched the

dust-raising cavalcade depart, the major with some satisfaction. With Mr Carlson's and José's descriptions of the *bandidos* he had almost a photograph of the men he had sworn to kill. And there was a good possibility of picking up their trail. Judgement Day for them, as Mr Carlson had pointed out earlier, was no longer just a fervent hope on his part. He turned and faced Buckskin.

'Mr Carlson,' he said, 'you have fulfilled your contract with me. I no longer need you to identify the men I seek. And, as I said, the actual killing of them is a personal matter, my and Alif's task. I thank you for all the help to me you have been. Now, if you would care to tell me what I owe you then you can take what supplies you need for your journey back to Arizona.'

'Why, you owe me nothin', Major,' Buckskin protested, somewhat taken aback at getting a sudden notice to quit. 'I ain't done nothin'. All I've been doin' is eatin' your chow for free.'

The major smiled. 'I haven't done

much either, Mr Carlson. Only Alif has earned his keep so far.'

'Don't you want me to go snoopin' into any villages again?' pleaded Buckskin, not prepared to be told to quit without a fight.

The major shook his head. 'As you probably heard me tell Don Argumedo, now that I feel we are within striking range of the bandits I have changed my tactics. I am hoping the bandits will find Alif and me. Having failed in their raid on the don's coach, they will think that two men, with pack animals, outlandishly dressed, to their way of thinking, will be, as you Westerners put it, 'easy pickings'.' The major's face hardened and Buckskin got the same fear-shivering feeling he had when eye-balling Chief Geronimo. 'Then, by thunder, Mr Carlson,' the major continued, 'they will have little time left to reflect on their mistake.'

Buckskin did a little reflecting on his own. The major was loco acting as a sitting duck for a bunch of bloodthirsty sons-of-bitches. And he must be just as crazy wanting to continue to ride with the coolest wild-asses he had ever known.

'As I said, Major,' he said. 'I don't want any payout. I oughta be payin' you, well, leastways, Alif, for soberin' me up. He kinda gave me my life back. It has been a privilege to have ridden alongside you and the big fella. I'd like to take my old mule with me, Major. Me and him have been pards for quite a spell, though he don't talk much about it.'

The major grinned. 'You take him, Mr Carlson. I wouldn't want to break up a long-standing friendship.'

* * *

With the mule loaded up with supplies and water, Buckskin, after handshakes with the major and Alif, headed north for the border.

'Mule,' Buckskin said, once well out of sight of his former partners, 'those

121

two *hombres* back there think we're makin' for Arizona, but we ain't. That big heathen is as good as any homegrown plainsman, or an Injun for that matter, but he could slip up. After all he ain't operatin' on his own ground. The major could just need another gun if things don't pan out for him.'

As Buckskin swung the mule's head round to ride along his back-trail it broke wind, loudly.

'Thanks for your backin',' he growled. 'I know I ain't a fearsome *pistolero* but I can handle a gun; I killed men durin' the War. Those two fellas gave me a purpose to live for; I'm beholden to them for that. So you keep your comments to yourself, mule, and just concentrate on movin' those big clumsy feet of yours real delicate like. If big Alif sees as much as a wisp of trail dust, he'll haul out his big cannon and blow me to hell and back. *Comprende*, pard? So move ass.'

7

A surly-faced Sam Pike sat in a cantina
that served the liquor needs of the male
inhabitants of a village comprising
several crumbling adobe buildings and
well-weathered, timber constructed shacks;
a comedown from the days and nights
of drinking, gambling and whoring in
Nogales he, Jesse Slade and the rest of
the Santos gang had indulged in when
their luck had been running high.

Jesse was sitting at the next table
playing poker with Primitivo, a thin-
shouldered Mexican with as much gold
showing in his mouth, Pike thought
sourly, that would make a panhandler
shout with joy if he had seen it rattling
around in his sieve. The stone-faced,
part Yaqui, Tomas, wasn't a drinking
man. He just sat there on his own with
a black cheroot stuck in his rat-trap of a
mouth. If the tip of the cheroot hadn't

glowed red regularly, the 'breed, thought Pike, could pass for a mummified corpse. Until it came to the killing time.

Santos was in a curtained-off corner of the cantina pleasuring a *señora* whom Pike opined was old enough to be Santos's mother.

Pike silently dirty-mouthed the gang's boss. It had been his crazy idea to raid the private coach, a raid that went against their normal tactics. Although Santos was only a shrimp-sized man, he made up for his small stature with a hair-trigger temper, willing to shoot down anyone who stood in his way, age or sex of no consequence. So, for his health's sake he had kept his doubts to himself. They had never taken on four heavily armed outriders before and counting the driver that made five men they had to kill fast before they were shot down. And there could have been armed men inside the coach. The more thought Pike had given to the proposed raid the less he liked about it.

'That coach isn't a regular stage, it's showing the coat of arms of a don,' Santos had told them. 'I think it's the mark of the don who owns the land north of here that stretches almost to the gringo border. What those escorts are guarding must be of great value, gold m'be for the don to buy some more gringo cattle?'

Pike had to admit that the little bastard could have been right; it *was* a big escort for one coach; it could have been hauling a box of gold. The gang had had some good pickings from their raids but they were all good spenders. In their line of business, saving up for old age wasn't an option. What they had raked in was quickly spent in the days and nights of high living in Nogales and soon they were looking around for fresh, unlawful ways to get rich again.

Pike did some more dirty-mouthing. So they had gone in shooting for Santos's 'gold'. Tomas with his arrows couldn't put down riders spread out all around the coach. But by hell, he thought, they had nearly pulled it off. The escorts had been taken by surprise. They had killed the driver and two of them without a shot being fired back. Then things started to go wrong. One of the goddamned escorts jumped on to the driver's box and grabbed hold of the reins and somehow drove the coach round the edge of the barricade of rocks they had sweated to lay on the trail and kept it rolling, rattling and bouncing across the open country.

Disappointed as he was, even the mad-ass Santos knew it was too dangerous to take off in hot pursuit. The dust of a Rurale patrol could show up at any time. The success of their previous raids had been the speed at which they had been carried out, with no one left alive to finger them. They had lost that edge now.

If they ever got rich again and rode into Nogales, they could be gazing on their likenesses on Wanted flyers. The price that would be posted on their heads, dead or alive, would have every two-bit, get-rich-quick *hombre* and bounty-hunter in Sonora on the look-out for them. Pike shivered. He wondered if the Rurales hanged captured *bandidos*, or shot them by firing squad. He wasn't about to sit in this rat-infested dump of a cantina drinking tequila that would rot the guts of a 'gator to find out. He looked across at Slade. After he had finished the game he would have words with him. Like, 'It's time we quit the gang and haul ass out of Sonora'.

8

A dust storm suddenly blew up, and to miss the worst of the skin-peppering blast, a coughing, red-eyed Buckskin kneed his mule down into a highsided arroyo that he opined must lead into the mountains through which Diablo Pass cut its way.

'It might take us a bit longer, mule, to get back on the heels of our late *amigos*,' he said, 'but it's better than endin' up wanderin' around in circles in that dust blizzard. Though all that dust flyin' about oughta shield us from the eagle-eyed Alif.'

Half a mile or so along the arroyo as it began to level out, the wind eased off allowing Buckskin to see a patch of clear blue sky and a beetling-faced mountain range, which meant he had judged right following the run of the wash. Then, before the dust storm cut off his vision again, Buckskin saw something that chilled his blood and set him cursing under his breath.

He had caught a glimpse of three half-naked riders, heads bowed against the storm, with bows slung across their backs. They could be Apache, Buckskin thought, but he wasn't gambling on them having got the word from their chief, Geronimo, that the Major and Alif had not to be harmed. He had a gut feeling that the bare-assed trio were Yaqui, hair-lifters who could teach the Apache a few things about inflicting pain on any Mexican or gringo unlucky enough to be captured by them. The major and Alif were in grave danger.

Buckskin tried to think positive thoughts, such as, though the Yaqui were riding in the direction of Diablo Pass if the storm continued they could ride within yards of the major and Alif and not see them. Buckskin didn't convince himself. The murdering sons-of-bitches could have already spotted them and were sneaking up on the pair.

The major and Alif wouldn't know they were about to be attacked until the dust storm died down, and shadowy, knife-wielding figures, whooping their death yells rushed them. And it would be too late for them to defend themselves.

Buckskin bared his teeth in a grimace of a smile. 'Mule,' he said, 'we ain't dogged renegade Injuns before, but we sure have to try, or that fine English gent and his big pard are goin' to end up dead, though not before they've suffered every pain a body being worked on by Yaquis can suffer.'

And so it would be likewise for him, Buckskin knew, if the storm lifted and one of the Yaquis looked over his shoulder and saw him, unless he was Dead-eyed Dick with his Winchester and could send the three of them to their happy hunting grounds before they got within feathered-stick range.

★　★　★

The major and Alif had reached the mouth of Diablo Pass and had dismounted at the rock barricade the *bandidos* had laid across the trail and Alif began to look for sign. Then the dust storm came howling in, turning daylight into darkness. The major's hopeful thoughts vanished with the light. What tracks the men they were seeking could have made were being blown away by the wind or covered by the dust.

He guided the horses into the shelter of some large boulders close to the pass face, calling on Alif to discontinue his searching before they lost sight of each other. A few minutes later Alif, puggaree unwound and wrapped round his face, rejoined him.

'The *badmash* rode south, Major *sahib*,' he said. 'The rest of their tracks are now lost.'

'Good work, my friend,' the major replied. 'But all is not lost, we have a direction to follow.' He gave a wry grin. 'Though it is a big unknown country southwards.'

The wind shifted again, and Buckskin found himself riding under a blazing sun. Ahead of him was the whirling smoky-grey wall and beyond it the higher real dark walls of the rocky bluffs of Diablo Pass.

A twanging-nerved Buckskin twisted ass in his saddle, looking wildly this way and everyway, his back twitching painfully as though a Yaqui arrow was already sticking in it. His quick glances around assured him that he was on his own. He cursed himself for acting like a frightened old maid. Somewhere in the dust haze in front of him were the major and Alif, two men who had given him back the reason for living again, and three murderous Yaquis breathing down their unsuspecting necks.

He drew out his Winchester and dismounted. 'Mule,' he said, stone-faced. 'It's a hard decision I've got to make, bein' you and me are pards and you stuck by me when I was nothin' but a drunken bum, and it would grieve me no end if you got stuck full of arrows, but there's two fine gents somewhere in that dust cloud and three butcherin' Yaqui gettin' set to jump them. I'm aimin' to send you fire-ballin' in, mule. Those big feet of yours stompin' across the rocks oughta alert the major and Alif, and get the Yaqui wonderin', m'be win me a little time so I can get in close with the Winchester and give my two ex-pards some back-up.'

Buckskin slapped the mule hard on its rump with the barrel of the Winchester. The mule showed its pain and hurt feelings in a lip-curling snort and broke into a gallop.

The major and Alif, crouching low behind a boulder, heard the loud clatter of iron-shod hooves in the narrow confines of the pass. They both straightened up, taut-nerved, the major drawing out his Webley, Alif yanking out his knife. They were veterans of wild frontiers and had to take it that any sound they heard could be made by men hostile to them. The dust storm began to abate somewhat, and shafts of sunlight broke through extending visibility to several yards, clear enough for both of them to see the low, bulky shape of a riderless mule race by them.

Alif let out a surprised grunt. It was the old man's mule. He looked questioningly at the major.

The major guessed wildly that Mr Carlson, by sending the mule through the pass, was warning them of some imminent danger about to befall them. He knew he could be wrong; Mr Carlson could be dead and the mule had just bolted this way. Guessing or not, he had always found it sound military tactics to prepare for the worst.

'I am taking it that that mule could have been sent in as a warning from Mr Carlson, Alif,' he said. 'If I am right, then it is not wise for us to stand here waiting for an unknown number of enemies rush us at any moment.' He wolf-smiled at Alif as he thumbed back the hammer of the pistol. 'We will do some rushing of our own.'

Alif gave him a curt acknowledging

nod and, getting a firmer grip on his knife, moved round the edge of the boulder away from the major.

The Yaquis had spotted the two gringos with the packhorses from afar. Grinning hopeful smiles that they would soon be lifting hated gringo scalps, and owners of four horses and many guns, they had dug their heels into their ponies' ribs, urging the animals into a gallop. They would swing round ahead of their intended victims so as to be lying in ambush as they entered the pass.

The dust storm forced them to pull back their ponies to a walking pace, and change their plan of attack. The Yaquis knew that the gringos would have to make camp until the storm cleared, allowing them the time to creep in on them under the cover of the storm and do their killing.

Alif slid on a patch of shale, stumbling forward a few paces: an accident that saved his life. The killing arrow only plucked at the sleeve of his thick coat. The Yaqui who had fired it followed in with his knife in his hand all worked up to scalp a fast dying man.

Alif saw the vague outline of a man hurtling at him from the rapidly clearing dust haze. He stepped forward, knife arm outstretched to meet the attack. He smelt the strong body sweat of his assailant as the momentum of his leap carried him on to the blade of the knife. Fierce grinning, Alif cut upwards with the big knife, hot sticky blood flooding over his wrist as he heard his attacker's painful gasping last breath. The dead Yaqui fell across his shoulder, Alif shrugged him off and he dropped to the ground, wiping his bloody hand and knife on his shirt. His eyes red with the killing lust, he listened and watched hard for his next attacker's movements.

The major heard the rattle of stones and spun round. The Webley bucked in his hand as he fired at the painted-faced Indian with his bow drawn at full stretch, poised on a rock above and behind him. He heard the Indian's deep cry of pain, then he dropped out of his sight.

The major's lips twitched in a slight smile. He had originally come to this land to hunt game, now the most dangerous game of all, a wild, fearless warrior, was hunting him. It was as though he had never left the regiment. And to cap it all his old leg wound was beginning to throb. Grimacing with the pain, he started to move forward, taking advantage of every covering rock and boulder now that the dust storm had all but settled: all his senses alert for sighting of the enemy, and wondering how many there were of them and how Alif was faring.

A sweating, out-of-breath Buckskin heard the shots. His plan seemed to have worked. At least the major hadn't been caught napping; that was the sound of his pistol he had just heard; he was putting up a fight. Then his face broke into an ear-stretching thankful grin as he caught sight of Alif sidling round the lip of a rocky tumble on the far side of the trail. 'There's three of the sons-of-bitches!' he yelled out. 'They ain't carryin' guns!'

Then he lost his smile for a twisted-faced look of pain as an arrow pierced the fleshy part of his leg. Groaning, he tottered round on one leg and fired the Winchester from across his hips at the Yaqui racing towards him howling like a banshee, wielding a stone-headed axe. The heavy calibre rifle shells fired at point-blank range hit the Yaqui full in the chest, stopped his war whooping dead and flung him backwards, arms outflung as though jerked by an unseen rope. Buckskin limped over to the body to make sure he had aimed true. He had heard tales of how seemingly 'dead' Indians came back to life to carry on with their killing.

The torn bloody mess that the Winchester shells had made of the Yaqui's chest confirmed to Buckskin that the Indian was beyond any hair-lifting this side of his happy hunting grounds. Only then did he bend down and with much cursing, pull out the arrow from his leg. Though the wound didn't bleed much he would have to cauterize it to prevent it going bad on him. He didn't want to die from a wound inflicted on him by a now dead Indian.

'Three of them you said, Mr Carlson?' the major shouted, his searching gaze sweeping over the rocks. 'I can account for one of them! Alif?'

'One, Major *sahib*.' Alif called back.

'Good, then we can stand down!' replied the major. 'And you can give Mr Carlson a hand to come in so we can attend to his wound.'

In long looping strides, Alif bounded across to Buckskin showing a smile Buckskin thought wasn't possible for such a stone-faced character. He felt a great surge of pride as Alif put his arm around him to take the weight off his wounded leg. The words *'Shabash, sahib,'* sounded double Dutch to him but he knew he was being thanked. Big

139

Alif and he were now genuine full-blooded partners.

The major smiled as they came up to him. 'It's thanks to you, Mr Carlson, and your mule,' he said, 'that Alif and I are not lying dead among these rocks. What decided you to come back?'

Buckskin grinned. He wouldn't have given a hoot if he had been punctured with a handful of arrows. 'Ah heck, Major,' he said. 'It didn't seem right for me to leave you two dudes wanderin' about on your ownsome in this troublesome territory.'

'I would appreciate it, Mr Carlson,' the major said, 'if you would condescend to act as our guide again. Think it over if you wish, but in the meantime sit down on that rock and allow Alif to tend to your wound.'

'It don't need no thinkin' over, Major,' Buckskin said. 'I never quit your service, you sorta fired me.'

'I did indeed, Mr Carlson,' the major replied. 'Though it was only to honour my agreement with you. Namely that

140

you had to take no part in any action Alif and I may take against the men we seek.'

'Yeah, well, that's m'be so, Major,' Buckskin said. 'But I'm agin that 'namely' bit. If it comes to a shoot-out with those *bandidos*, I'm your third gun. OK, Major?'

'OK, Mr Carlson,' the major said. He grinned and took Buckskin's hand in a firm handshake. 'Welcome to the Hellfire Club. Alif, do your healing. I do not wish to be trapped in this gorge by any comrades of those fellows we killed. We will bury them before we leave.'

'Raisin' a sweat to bury butcherin' Injuns, Major!' Buckskin gasped. 'Why, why, it just ain't done!'

'Those Indians may well have been butchering savages, Mr Carlson,' replied a sombre-faced major, 'from the whites' point of view. From their standpoint they are fighting a war against us the only way they know how. And I fight my wars my way and that includes, if time and conditions allow, burying the enemy dead.'

After Buckskin had had his wound seen to and while the major and Alif were covering the Yaquis' bodies with stones, he borrowed Alif's horse to see if he could find his mule.

'I know you're in a hurry, Major, to start searchin', so I won't go more than a mile or so along the pass,' he said. 'I figure the stubborn critter will be standin' there sulkin' just a piece along the trail. I ain't about to leave him to be set upon by mountain cats, or taken by the Yaqui or some Mex and worked to death, He's the only family I've got, Major.'

'By all means do that, Mr Carlson,' the major said. 'That critter as you put it, saved my and Alif's lives. He has earned his place in our small fighting force.'

* * *

When the 'fighting force' moved out, a slightly stiff-legged Buckskin was

142

mounted on a horse once again, and had as strong a sense of purpose to gun down the *bandidos* as the major and Alif. His mule, now loaded with supplies, trotted along contentedly behind him.

9

'Another goddamned dog-dirt dump, Pike,' Slade growled. 'There ain't anything here to line our pockets worth steppin' down from our horses for.' He scowled at Pike. 'You ain't thinkin' of goin' into that rathole of a cantina and pistol-whippin' the greaser owner and robbing him of his few pesos in takin's?'

The pair had finally quit Santos's gang and were heading for the Arizona border and were riding across Mexican territory unknown to them in their raiding days with Santos. And being very low in the financial stakes, they had been hoping to ride into a small Mexican town that boasted a bank, or at least a well-stocked general store where with the threat of drawn guns they could get their hands on some easy ready cash to bankroll them for a week or two once they were back on

American soil. The last thing either of them wanted to do was to start their robbing ways as soon as they crossed over into Arizona and bring the law down on them before they knew their way around the territory.

Pike and Slade hadn't actually told Santos they were quitting the gang. There hadn't been any handshakes and back-slapping and wishes of good luck from Santos and their Mexican partners in crime. While Santos, Tomas and Primitivo were sleeping off a heavy night's drinking, they gathered what little gear they had, saddled up their mounts, and rein-led them well away from the camp before mounting up to ride north for the border, both knowing that Santos's farewells to them would be several pistol shells in their backs.

While Pike had already made up his mind to quit the gang the first chance he got, when he had had words with Slade to see if he would ride with him, Slade had turned him down. Slade wasn't happy staying with the gang, but he stood by the old adage of better-ride-with-the-devil-you-know than risk riding with Pike across territory occupied by real unfriendly red devils which two guns could not hold off if they ran into them. Santos's latest plan to make his *muchachos* rich again changed his mind and he was willing to risk exchanging lead with the Yaqui.

'We will rob Don Carlos Argumedo's fine hacienda, *compadres*,' he had said. At first, Slade thought that Santos was ribbing them, but his wild tequila-inflamed eyes showed no humour; craziness, definitely. He noticed that Pike was as amazed as he was at Santos's suggestion.

'But the don has a whole army of tough, fast-shooting *vaqueros*, Santos,' he said. 'We'll never get within a coupla miles of the house before the sonsuvbitches shoot us down. Some of them are part Injun; they'll be able to smell us out.'

'As you say, *amigo*,' Santos said. 'The don has many *vaqueros* but they guard his cattle and many fine horses.'

Santos's death's head mask of a face twisted in a fearsome smile. 'The riches we seek are in the hacienda and only *pacifico* servants will be in there. We go in on foot, silently, like the Yaqui.'

Slade's mind briefly dwelt on the riches that would be in a big shot don's house: gold, silver, jewellery, handed down from grandpappy to father then son. Then he thought of the dozens of *vaqueros* the don had on his payroll, Indian blood hunters who would show them no mercy if caught. Death would come by the bullet or rope if they so much as smelt them. Of this Slade was sure, as if someone had put it in writing for him. Pike's idea of quitting the gang sounded real good, if he wanted to stay alive.

Now here they were, he thought sourly, alive all right but in another stinking, piss-poor greaser village.

'Hey, Slade,' he heard Pike say. 'This dump has a mission. We may be in luck. Some of these Mex churches have rich pickin's such as gold or silver crosses and plates the peons find buried in the caves in the hills. The dumb bastards ain't got no more sense but to hand them over to the village priest to decorate his church with. They think it'll guarantee a better place in Heaven.' He grinned wolfishly at Slade. 'M'be the Good Lord is about to smile on two hardened sinners. Let's go and have a look.' And he swung down from his saddle.

Slade wasn't as optimistic as his pard about the possible riches lying in the church for them to grab as he trailed after Pike towards the mission. What he could see of the building it didn't seem to hold any pieces of gold and silver. The adobe walls were pock-marked with age; it looked as though it had been under prolonged cannon fire. He spat in the dust. They would be richer robbing the cantina.

Father Castro was carrying out his everlasting penance since he had taken over the mission — sweeping the porch

148

clear of the throat-choking sand and dust he was convinced El Diablo had blown here every day just to test his faith. He heard the jangle of spurs behind him and that puzzled him for a moment or two. It was very rare for any *vaqueros* from the big haciendas to pay a visit to the village. Knowing the weaknesses of men, he grinned slightly. There wasn't much here in the way of the sins of the flesh to satisfy a hard-working, red-blooded *vaquero*. His grin broadened into a welcoming smile as he turned to greet his unexpected visitors.

Father Castro's smile stiffened as he found himself gazing at two merciless-eyed, unshaven gringos. He had no doubts that they were *bandidos*. He muttered a silent prayer, forcing himself to keep smiling.

'*Buenos dias, señors*,' he said. 'Welcome to my humble mission.'

Pike's smile did nothing to allay Father Castro's fears that the two gringos were *mal hombres*.

'Yeah, and a welcome to you, padre,' Pike said. 'We'd like to take a peek inside your church. I figure it ain't so humble inside as it is outside. In fact, my pard here will be right put out if there ain't any pieces of gold and silver on show.'

Father Castro gave Pike an incredulous look and even found enough courage to laugh back at him. 'Gold and silver, *señor*? Look around you, at the walls, the roof! Does it look as though I have precious altar cups and plates? Someone has misinformed you, *señor*.'

Slade gave Pike a fish-eyed glare. 'What did I tell you, Pike?' he grated. 'This place ain't got enough cash floatin' around to buy a hatful of grain for our horses.'

Pike stepped forward and rammed his pistol under Father Castro's chin, forcing his head back until he heard the priest cry out in pain.

'We'll go inside and take a look for ourselves, padre,' he snarled. 'And if we find you're foolin' us, that you've got some fine pieces tucked away some place then you'll be on your way to meet up with St Peter sooner than you expected.'

Pike grabbed Father Castro with his left hand and spun him round. Then with a barked, 'Let's go then!', jabbed his pistol in the priest's back and propelled him forward.

The rough hewn wooden table covered by a faded, ragged cloth that did service as an altar, the crumbling plaster on the walls, the shafts of sunlight streaming through several places in the roof, and Pike seeing two earthenware vases, one filled with drooping-headed desert flowers standing on the table where he had hoped to see gold and silver plates, caused him to think that Slade had been right, there was nothing here they could turn into spending money. It had been a waste of time getting off their horses.

Boiling over with anger and a feeling of being cheated, a dirty-mouthing Pike shot Father Castro in the back, shocking the stone-hearted Slade, who had gunned down women and old men in his attempts to get rich quick. He looked down at the priest's body lying arms outstretched in front of his altar, and the spreading dark stain on the back of his cloak.

Somewhere in the deep, dark recesses of his mind, a tiny spark of old-time religion still flickered. To kill a priest in his church for no material gain was a killing he would have balked at.

He glared at Pike. 'Let's get to hell outa this dog-dirt village! Your god-damned stupidity has labelled us as priest killers. We'll be hounded all the way to the border! And for damn all recompense!'

Pike shot Slade a mad-eyed look, holding his pistol on him. 'I ain't leaving this place until we get us at least some supplies. Then we ass-kick it nonstop to the border well ahead of any hunt comin' along our back-trail.' Pike steadied his gun on Slade and gave him a mirthless grin. 'Unless you have a different idea, pard?'

Slade's throat dried up with fear. He didn't want to end up dead alongside the priest. And pard or not, Pike would gun him down as unfeelingly as he had done the priest. 'Naw, I ain't got any plans of my own, Pike,' he croaked. 'Except that we make it quick collectin' in the supplies.'

★　★　★

The three *bandido* hunters had been favoured with a stroke of good luck. Buckskin, to prove his worth to the major after his rehiring, had been bird-dogging the ground well wide of the regular trail they were riding along and, in a stretch of softer ground, had seen several horse tracks that brought a triumphant smile to his face. Alif had told him that the track of the horses he had picked up before the storm broke, showed that one of their mounts had a loose left-rear shoe. The tracks he had got off his horse to examine more closely, showed he was seeing that loose shoe for himself. The tracks were leading well to the west of the small village just ahead of them.

The faint single crack of a firearm from the village had the three of them looking questioningly at each other.

'That sounds like a pistol shot, Major,' Buckskin said.

'Do you think it could have been fired by one of the men we are trailing, Mr Carlson?' the major said, all alert.

'I dunno,' replied Buckskin. 'It could be. They could have for some reason or other changed their minds and cut across to the village after all. All I do know is it's most unlikely that a Mex villager pulled off that shot.' He grinned at the major. 'I reckon it's time I did my lonesome drifter routine and checked things out over there. If it's the killers we're after who are over there, Major, then we don't want to kinda barge in on them, seein' that there's five of them, all experts in the killin' business.'

The major shook his head. 'Not this time, Mr Carlson,' he said, grim-faced. 'We all ride in. If it is the men we seek, we may never get this close to them again. Five killing men or not, the odds are in our favour. We will be innocent travellers in their eyes and before they can think up a plan to rob us without any danger to themselves, they'll be dead. After all, Mr Carlson we are not exactly inexperienced in the killing business, are we?' The major's smile was as hard as his look.

As they approached the village they heard the tolling of the mission bell and several villagers running across to the church. The major wondered what religious feast day was being celebrated when he saw two men carrying what seemed to be a dead, or badly wounded man from out of the church. By his garb he looked like a padre.

'It wasn't just a random pistol shot we heard, Mr Carlson,' he said. 'It would be prudent to see to our own well-being.' He drew out his Webley and held it down by his right side. Alif unslung the Snider and laid it across the front of his saddle, cocking hammer thumbed back. Buckskin, guessing that his moment of truth could be almost upon him, pulled the Winchester out of its boot and levered a shell into the chamber. Trouble that got within pistol range was trouble too close for his peace of mind.

The peons at the church scattered for the safety of their houses as they caught sight of the three riders closing in on them, leaving only one elderly man standing beside the unceremoniously discarded body of Father Castro. The old man took a firmer grip on the machete he wielded, and glared up at the leading rider, his anger overcoming his fear of the three heavily armed men.

'Are you the *jefe* of those gringo dogs who have killed our priest?' he asked defiantly.

The major looked down at the grey-grizzled, age-etched face. 'I am not, *señor*,' he replied, sombre-voiced.

'No one in your village has anything to fear from us. In fact our mission in your land is to hunt down *bandidos*. Where are those gringo *bandidos* now, and do they ride with Mexican *bandidos*?'

A much relieved village elder lowered his machete. By the manner of his speech the white man wasn't a cursed *bandido*, but he had the commanding features of a *jefe* of some sorts. The big hooked-nose rider next to him holding a rifle as long as the length a man could stretch both of his arms was an *hombre* he had never seen the like before and who, in spite of the white man's words of peace, still frightened him. But he believed the promise that they had no bad thoughts against his village was true.

'Two gringos only, *señor*,' he said. 'And they are in the cantina, yonder.' He pointed with his machete to a long building on the far side of the village well.

Two. The major's spirits were dampened. Maybe, he thought, he had been hoping too much, expecting to be told that the Americans were accompanied by three of the old man's countrymen. Disappointed or not, he knew he could not leave the villagers to be terrorized by two brutal killers. While he also knew Alif would follow him if he told him he was riding to Hell to fight the Devil, Mr Carlson would have to be given the choice of leaving his service. He had offered his expertise for a specific task not to liberate from death and fear every Mexican village they came across. He told Buckskin of his decision then asked his guide if he was in agreement with it.

Buckskin gave him a lopsided grin. 'Major,' he said, 'when I set on this trail I sure didn't think it meant that we would be killin' every bad man in Sonora, but it's lookin' like that and if that's the only way we can reach those fellas we're chasin' then that's the way it's gotta be. And while I'm in a real talkin' mood I think it's wiser for me to go to that cantina on my own. A terrible thing has been done here, Major, the killing of a priest, but that don't mean we oughta go at things half-cock. We could get ourselves killed which would still leave those two sonsuvbitches in the cantina alive and the *bandidos* we're huntin' still doin' their raidin'.'

The major gave what his guide had said some thought before saying, 'You are absolutely right, Mr Carlson. If they have spotted us we can no longer pass ourselves off as innocent travellers. They will know that we are aware of their killing of the priest and will do their utmost to do likewise to us. Not just for what riches we have, guns, horses and the like, but to silence us as witnesses to their crime. He close-eyed Buckskin. 'That doesn't make it any easier for you, Mr Carlson, does it? You'll be the first of us they will try to kill.'

'I was tryin' not to think of that, Major,' Buckskin replied with a bold-assed smile he was putting on for Alif's benefit. 'But I'm hopin', bein' that it's the back of the cantina facin' us, those two wild boys ain't seen us. If they have' — Buckskin shrugged — 'then I'll have to do some fast movin' to stop them from pluggin' me. That oughta give you and Mr Alif time to come up with some sorta plan to get the drop on them.'

The major grinned. 'Mr Carlson, you would have fitted in well with my Afridis. Why damnit, they probably would have made you their blood brother in spite of you being a *Feringhi* infidel. You go and pay a call on those two across the way; Alif and I will be nearby, never fear.' Silently, the major promised himself that if the worst came to the worst, Mr Carlson would be the last man who would fall to the priest killers' guns.

Buckskin rode slowly towards the cantina, thinking that his new-found pride in himself was getting a mite out of hand. It was an unreal cocksure attitude that could get him killed within the next few minutes. Yet somehow it didn't seem to worry him. Which had him puzzling whether it was possible to be crazy drunk without partaking of strong liquor.

Buckskin wasn't that overcome by his need to prove his mettle to the major and Alif not to take any precautions for his safety. He stopped just short of accurate rifle range from the cantina and dismounted and began fiddling with his saddle straps all the while casting furtive glances at the open door of the cantina. He eased out his rifle from its boot until it would only take a matter of a second or two to pull it all the way out, aim, and fire it. He had also positioned himself in line with the two tethered horses outside the cantina which meant he couldn't come under fire from the only window in the front wall. If the gunmen wanted to take potshots at him they would have to do it from the open doorway. Buckskin reckoned he had done all he could to swing things in his favour. What happened next would have to be played the way it came.

A tequila wound-up Pike came out of the cantina. He felt mad enough to have shot a whole churchful of greaser priests. As Slade had forecast, the cantina held no stocks of supplies, and the takings only yielded enough pesos to buy a few reloads, or a sack of grain for their horses. Other than ransacking every flea-ridden shack in the village, he could see no way of becoming any richer. As soon as Slade had relieved himself out back they would get to hell out of this dump and not stop riding until they had crossed over the border.

It took Pike a few seconds for his eyes to adjust to the searing glare of the sun and to see the horse and its dismounted rider. Pike grinned wolf-ishly. Selling the horse and its gear once they crossed the border would raise him and Slade a good few dollars. Enough for them to study the lie of the land, peace-officer wise, before taking up their killing and robbing again. Though the old fart who owned the horse had to be despatched first, which ought to be no sweat-raising task.

'Howdee, *amigo*!' he called out, as he walked over to his unexpected windfall. 'It's a real pleasure to see a Yankee face in this goddamed hell-hole of a land.'

All of Buckskin's nerve ends twanged painfully. He had seen the gunman walking towards him before. Saw him pumping shells into a coachful of passengers, one of them the major's sister. The villagers had told them there were only two gringos involved in the shooting of the priest. If the three Mexicans in the gang were nearby then the major and Alif would have to keep a good watch out when the shooting started. And it was going to start soon. The evil-smiling bastard coming towards him would see to that. Buckskin's hand stopped fumbling with the strap buckle and sneaked down to his pistol stuck in the top of his pants.

Pike didn't see the move, but something in the old man's face made him realize his outward show of friendliness hadn't paid off. Cursing he grabbed for his gun.

Buckskin stepped back a pace from his horse, half-turned to face his attacker and fired his pistol across his belly, in his panicky haste emptying all the chambers, the muzzle flashes burning an acrid smoking hole in his coat. He didn't know how many of his wild shots had hit his target, but he saw the *bandido* stagger backwards slightly then fall heavily to the ground to lie there as unmoving as a felled tree. Buckskin was confident that if he hadn't killed him he was no longer a threat. But his partner back there in the cantina was. He drew out the Winchester and levered a shell in the chamber, then, half-crouched, laid the sights on the open doorway. Not since the war had he been in a killing mood but he was in one now. If the son-of-a-bitch so much as poked his nose through the door he was a dead man.

Slade had slipped his suspenders back over his shoulders and was buttoning up his flies when he heard the shooting and wondered what greaser the mad-ass Pike was shooting lumps out of. He gave out a sharp cry of pain as his head was jerked back. He saw a knife, as long as a horse soldier's sabre, then felt the cold sharp steel prick at his exposed throat. A tear-filled-eyed Slade felt the overwhelming need to drop his pants and have another crap. Dimly he heard a voice say, 'Hold him there, Alif, kill him if necessary. I'll go and see how Mr Carlson's faring.'

Slade stayed held, hardly daring to breathe.

With pistol drawn and cocked, the major walked into the cantina. He slipped quickly to one side as soon as he stepped into the building. On the frontier where he had been blooded, a man showing himself in an open doorway for more than a few seconds was asking for a sniper's bullet in his stupid head. A quick glance around the dark interior of the cantina assured the major that the place was deserted. He moved across to the back door and risked a glance out, and saw a body lying on the ground and Mr Carlson pointing a rifle directly at him.

'Put up your gun, Mr Carlson!' he called out, and came out into the open. 'Alif is holding that fellow's companion. The business here is ended.'

Buckskin straightened up, his blood lust rapidly cooling and leaving him with shaky limbs. He reckoned he was a long ways off from being a shootist, even though he had killed a hard-assed *bandido*.

'Major,' he said excitedly, as the major came up to him. 'That sonuvabitch lyin' there is one of the gang who killed your sister. Alif must be holdin' the other gringo in the gang. What we've got to worry about is where are the three Mexes?' His nervous gaze swept all parts of the village.

The major looked back at the body. 'Are you sure, Mr Carlson?'

'I'm sure,' replied Buckskin. 'I'll

remember those five murderous bastards' faces if I live to be a hundred.'

'Then we will have to ask our prisoner where the rest of the gang is, Mr Carlson,' the major said.

The villagers came out of their houses once they saw that the gringo *bandidos* were no longer a threat to them. Two of them, at the request of the major, passed on to them by the village elder, were in the mission bell tower scanning for signs of trail dust that could herald the coming of the three Mexican *compadres* of the gringos who had killed their priest.

After taking their priest's body into the church and laying it on the altar, most of the inhabitants gathered round the captive Slade, eye-balling the big fearsome *hombre* whose race they couldn't figure out, holding in awe the great, broad-bladed knife he kept flashing in front of the *bandido's* fear-twisted face.

'Where are those three Mexicans, the other members of your gang?'

questioned the major. 'One of them is the leader. What is his name? I repeat, where are they now?'

Slade knew that if he confessed to having been one of Santos's gang with all the killings and robberies they had carried out, he risked being shot, or hanged out of hand by the prissy speaking dude, who, he opined, could only be a bounty-hunter. Here there was only a dead priest to answer for and that had been Pike's work. If he kept his head he could get out of this situation alive.

Licking dry lips he croaked, 'I ain't a member of any gang bossed over by a Mex, mister. Me and Pike, the fella the old man there shot, only stopped here to see if we could pick up any loose change, so to speak, to tend to our needs on our ride back to the border. Then that goddamned Pike had to go and kill the priest.'

'Do not play the innocent with us,' the major snapped. 'We are well aware of who you and your dead companion are. That 'old man' knows the description of all the members of the gang you rode with. On one of your raids, you murderous swine killed my sister!'

The major's voice no longer sounded prissy to Slade, it gave him the shakes.

The major gave Alif a curt nod.

The big Kabuli knife flashed up and passed across Slade's throat, leaving a trickling red line on the flesh in its wake, causing even Buckskin to wince and to think that the big man was enjoying his work. The knife came back for another slicing and too petrified with fear to scream, Slade cracked as a dark, damp patch spread over the front of his pants.

'The fellas you want are Santos, Primitivo and Tomas!' the words came babbling out. 'Santos runs the gang! When me and Pike left them, Santos was fixin' to raid a rich don's hacienda some miles north of here. He reckons that a private coach that slipped by us must be carrying something valuable on account of the armed riders escortin' it.

He figures what riches it was carryin' are still at this hacienda. Where the three are right now, your guess is as good as mine!' Slade looked pleadingly at the major. 'That's all I can tell you, mister, I swear!'

Then Slade's self-preservation instincts conquered a little of his fears. As bold-voiced as he could, he said, 'I reckon that information is kinda like me turnin' state's evidence. It oughta keep you from seein' me hanged.'

The major's face boned over as he thought of the riches the coach had carried. By the grace of God the young *señorita* had escaped death, or worse, by Santos's hands. This time she might not be so fortunate. Still deep in thought he said, 'I have no intention of seeing you hang.'

Slade's heart began to beat somewhat more regularly. Maybe he had pissed his pants and was flat broke, but that was a long ways better than having his neck stretched, or shot down like poor Pike. He had a good feeling he was going to make it to the border after all. Then he saw the hard Indian-faced look the dude was giving him. His good feeling vanished: he would get no nearer to the border than Pike had. His bladder began to play up again.

The major turned to the village elder. '*Señor*,' he said 'I will give you the privilege of despatching this *bandido* to Hell. As you have just heard, *bandidos* are going to raid the Hacienda La Carendo. It is urgent I ride to warn them of their danger.' If it is not too late, he thought. 'Can you do that duty?' he added.

'We will do that, *señor*,' the old Mexican replied. 'We've a stout tree and a strong rope. We will even hang the dead gringo and leave them both hanging as a warning to any others who would try to rob our village. You and your *compadres* ride at once to the hacienda. Ride with the good wishes of our village, *señor*.'

The old man glared fiercely at Slade, spat out some orders in Mexican and several peons, with yells of triumph, rushed at Slade and carried him away bodily, kicking and screaming.

'We have made a good start,' the major said. 'Two to be crossed off our list, gentlemen. Are we ready to ride, Mr Carlson? Have we sufficient water for us and the horses?'

'We're only waitin' for the order to mount up, Major,' Buckskin said. 'But I suggest leavin' our pack animals here, they'll slow us down.'

'Good idea, Mr Carlson,' the major said: 'See to it. We don't know how much time we have got, so it is going to be one mad gallop.'

A kicking and writhing Slade was gasping for his last few seconds of life-giving air before the distant trail dust of the three *amigos* of the village had completely drifted away, and as the village elder had told the gringo *jefe*, the vengeful peons hauled the body of the shot *bandido* up on the branches alongside the still swinging body of his *compadre*.

Then they saw to it that their murdered priest was reverently laid to rest. The village elder had another duty that needed carrying out. He called out two names and two peons stepped forward and he gave them their orders.

10

They had ridden hard for an hour or so since leaving the village across arid, flat land which seemed to the major's experienced eyes clear of any danger to them. They even kept up their horses' ground-eating pace when on their left the trail began to parallel a low rocky ridge though their ever-watchful eyeing of the way ahead sharpened. The major knew he was forsaking sound military principles in moving a small force headlong across unknown, hostile territory. A risk he was, and he believed Alif and Mr Carlson also were willing to accept if it meant the saving of a young girl's life. Speed and luck, he hoped, would see them through unscathed to the Hacienda La Carendo.

The major didn't hear the shot that killed his horse. The first thing he knew that luck and speed weren't going to work for them was his horse sinking suddenly beneath him, flinging him over its head to land with such force on to the ground that he felt the snap and sickening pain of a broken forearm. Then he heard the crack of rifle shots from the rocks above him and saw the ominous spurts of dust being kicked up around him of near misses. He flattened himself into the contours of the land.

Alif and Buckskin yanked up their horses in a haunch-sliding halt and leapt out of their saddles. 'Get the major under cover, Alif!' Buckskin yelled. 'I'll see to the horses!'

Before Alif got to the major, Gaunt called out, 'I'm all right. Alif! Let's get dug in and let whoever it is who's firing at us know that we have teeth!'

'I've counted four rifles, Major,' Buckskin said. The three of them were lying in a frantically hand-scraped hollow behind a hastily thrown-up parapet of rocks, allowing them to raise their heads a few inches. Risking a clearer sighting of their attackers' positions would be asking to be killed. Though that did not prevent a fierce scowling Alif firing the Snider between the rocks, growling something in Pushtu, that Buckskin took to be curse words in the big man's language, when the wailing, heavy slugs only chipped splinters of rock from his target's position.

'And they are only using single-shot rifles, Mr Carlson,' the major said. 'If they possessed Winchester repeating rifles we would all have been swept out of our saddles before we knew we had ridden into an ambush. I take it they are Yaquis.'

'More than likely, Major,' replied Buckskin. 'Yaqui and Apache war trails leading up to the border are as well used as regular turnpikes. And even if the sonsuvbitches had repeaters they wouldn't have had any intention of tryin' to put us all down in one blaze of gunfire. They could kill all the horses that way. Now they're thinkin' they've got themselves two horses and when the light goes, three *hombres* to roast over a fire to while the night away.'

Buckskin took in the major's pain-drawn face and the way he was holding his left arm. 'Have you busted your arm, Major?' he asked, in a concerned voice.

'It feels like it, Mr Carlson,' the major said. 'But that's neither here nor there.' He looked up at the sun. 'It will be dark in a couple of hours and that's when Santos and his fellow butchers will raid the don. One of us has to make it to the hacienda to warn them, if it is not already too late.' The major had never been a worrying man however black the situation seemed, until now that is. And the situation couldn't be much darker. He could do nothing to save his sister's life, but he would try his damnedest to save the young *señorita* from suffering the same fate. He gave Buckskin a long, hard look.

'That will have to be you, Mr Carlson,' he said. 'If you are willing to do so; it is not part of your contract. I can't ride with one hand and Alif, by the way he's cursing, won't leave this spot until he has drawn some Yaqui blood.' The major smiled thinly. 'I'll have to be satisfied with only bringing two of my sister's killers to account, Mr Carlson. Looking realistically at the task I had set myself, two is more than I could have hoped to achieve. I'll ask Alif to cover you with the Winchester.'

'I'll go, Major,' a grim-faced Buckskin said, without any hesitation. He was feeling the loss of the major's sister as though she had been kin to him. 'And I'll do my best to hunt down those three Mexican sons-of-bitches;' he added, under his breath, not wanting to sound like some blowhard. He hadn't got clear of the Yaqui ambushers yet. Though he had been given a chance to stay alive. The major and Alif would be dead come nightfall.

The major laid his good hand on Buckskin's shoulder for a moment or two. 'Good man,' he said. 'Alif and I are proud to have had you fighting alongside us, Mr Carlson.' His smile this time held more warmth. 'You can't fail to make it to the hacienda, Mr Carlson. I am wishing you Godspeed and I have no doubts that Alif will pray to his God, Allah, to look kindly on you.'

Buckskin grinned embarrassedly. 'Yeah, well, I'll be sayin' a few prayers of my own, Major.' He grinned. 'I ain't fussy what god, saint, whoever, runs things up there as long as they keep me ridin' well ahead of any bare-assed, hair-liftin' pursuers.'

Buckskin began to worm his way to the cluster of rocks on the far side of the trail to where the horses were. Alif, shouting something in his own tongue before he had made it out of the hollow stopped his painful, nerve-racking progress. He looked over his shoulder and saw that Alif and the major were leaning across the rock barricade looking up at the bluff. Buckskin turned and scrambled back over to them.

179

The major grinned at him. 'Some Good Samaritan has come to our aid, Mr Carlson! See!' he pointed upwards.

Higher and to the left of where the Yaqui had been firing down on them, Buckskin heard the crack of two rifles and twin spurts of muzzle smoke as they cut loose at the Yaqui. He didn't know if it was his prayers that had been answered, or if Alif's Allah had looked favourably on them, as he saw the Yaqui leave their bushwhacking positions and began rock-hopping across the face of the bluff.

'By thunder, Major!' he cried. 'The sonsuvbitches are high-tailin' it!' He let out a war whoop as one of the Yaqui seemed to stumble and came rolling down the slope in a flurry of dirt and stones.

Alif let out his battle howl. There was now a chance to die like an Afridi, not like some stinking pi-dog grovelling in the dust. Along the North-West Frontier, a man was judged not by what he had achieved in life, but how manly had he died, and how many of his enemies he had taken with him. He discarded the Winchester and picked up the Snider. Its booming roar rattled around the high ridges, echoed by a thin, dying wail from one of the three remaining Yaqui before he dropped out of sight. Buckskin brought his Winchester up to his shoulder to join in the turkey shoot.

Only one Yaqui escaped the deadly crossfire, vanishing in a cleft in the bluff face. In the silence that followed, a wide-smiling major took off his hat and waved it at the still unseen riflemen. It was acknowledged by a waved sombero as two Mexicans stood up from behind a ridge.

Buckskin noticed that Alif wasn't leaving things as they were. With his rifle held at the long trail, he was looping up the bluff as sure-footed as a mountain goat to check on the shot Yaqui, ready, he knew, to despatch them to hell if they weren't already on their way there with the big pig-sticker he held in his right hand. Which made

Buckskin opine that where the big man came from, his enemies were also sneaky enough to play possum in the hope of getting in a unexpected killing stroke.

The major stepped over the barricade to greet the two Mexicans as they picked their way down to the trail. He shook both peons' hands with some feeling when they came up to him.

'My friends,' he said 'your timely intervention saved our lives and we thank you for doing so.'

'We are from the village, *señor*,' the elder of the Mexicans said. 'We were honour bound to come to your aid. I am called Obregon, my *compañero* is named Fabelo. We have brought your pack animals. Vallejo, the village elder, said that you would need your supplies if you have to start tracking the *bandidos* you seek and you can ill afford the time to ride back to the village to collect them.'

'It was wise thinking on your village elder's part, Señor Obregon,' the major said. 'But you have done more than just bring us our supplies; as I said, you have saved our lives and have given us the chance, which I thought we had lost, to warn Don Argumedo of the danger he and his family are in.' The major keen-eyed Obregon. He smiled. 'You have the cut of an old soldier about you, *señor*,' he said. 'Only a soldier would have picked such dominant firing positions.'

Old Obregon stiffened his shoulders. Proud-faced, he said, 'I was a sergeant in the Juarista army, *señor*,' he replied. He looked at Buckskin. 'I was what they call in your army, a sharpshooter.'

'Juarez, Major, was the *hombre* who led the fight against the Spanish to win Mexico for the Mexicans,' Buckskin said.

A single rifle shot high up on the bluff stopped their conversation and had the four of them whirling round to look up at the high ground.

'That sounds like Mr Alif's big gun, Major,' Buckskin said. 'I hope he ain't run into Yaqui trouble.' He brought his Winchester up into a firing position.

'I don't think so, Mr Carlson,' replied the major. 'Some Yaqui could have run into trouble. Mr Alif does not generally fire his Snider at anyone whom he hasn't got a fair chance of killing or disabling. Ah, here he comes now. What trouble that shot signified seems to have been resolved, in Alif's favour.'

Alif came down from the high places as sure footed as he had climbed the bluff, sliding on the loose shale to speed his descent. Just by looking at the big man's face as he came nearer, Buckskin found it hard to believe that he had climbed up and down a steep rock face with some speed, sought out a deadly enemy when he got up there among the ridges and killed him. Only the dark patches of sweat on his shirt and the slight mad glint in the narrow slits of eyes showed that it hadn't been an evening stroll for Alif. Though the deadpan announcement of, 'All dead, Major *sahib*,' almost made Buckskin think it had been.

'Good show, Alif,' the major said. 'Now we can carry on with our mission to alert Don Argumedo of the threat. But first I must introduce you to the two stalwarts, Señors Obregon and Fabelo who, by their bold actions, have made that possible.'

Alif eyed the older Mexican that much longer, recognizing in his bearing a former soldier. 'You attacked with the skill of an Afridi,' he said. 'And made your kill.'

Neither Obrengo of Fabelo knew who the Afridi were but if the big stranger was one, then the Afridi must be a tribe of fierce warriors, ranking with the fearsome Yaqui and Apache. And they were being praised as equals to the fierce-looking killer of *bandidos*. They would both have something to talk about to the other villagers in the cantina when they returned to the village.

'There is one other great service you can do us, *señors*,' the major said. 'I need a horse; as you can see mine has been shot dead.'

'Take mine, *señor*,' Obregon said. He grinned. 'I am more used to walking than riding. It is only right that a dead *bandido*'s horse should be used to kill others. You ride with all speed, *señor*, we will follow your trail with the packhorses.'

Within minutes, the major, his broken arm strapped up, was being helped into the saddle by Alif. He thanked Obregon and Fabelo again for coming to their aid, then issued one last order before digging his heels into his horse's flanks.

'If you see me lagging behind, Mr Carlson,' he said. 'You ride on. Warning the don is more important than my well-being, understand?'

For a real English dude, Buckskin thought, if he hadn't already known, the major was as hard-assed as they came. Straight-faced he replied, 'Understood, Major.'

11

Tomas, lying behind a low ridge as unmoving as a basking rattler, watched all that was taking place at the Hacienda La Carendo. He had been doing so since an hour before dawn so he had seen the four hacienda night guards and mentally marked their patrol boundaries.

The three had ridden on to Don Argumedo's land in the early hours of a pitch-dark night. Far away to their left and right, they could make out the red pinpricks of the fires of the *vaqueros* standing guard over the vast herds of their *jefe's* Texas longhorns. Santos knew they were in no danger of being seen by any of the *vaqueros*, the vastness of the don's holdings was working in their favour. It would need the whole Mexican Army to prevent any intruder from trepassing on his land. Santos smiled to himself. Anyone that is but a Yaqui, or the 'breed Tomas.

Santos, though eager to get his hands on the riches he believed were stowed in the don's fine house, was not foolishly risking his and his *muchachos'* lives. If the alarm was raised, the don could count on fifty, maybe sixty *vaqueros* to rally to his call. The three of them would be run down and shot to pieces. He lifted his hand for them to halt, as a rising wind began to break up the thick clouds, allowing, he judged, in a few minutes' time, the high, bright moon to shine through and light up the land as if it was daylight.

'Tomas,' he said. 'Find us a place where we can make camp, pronto.'

Tomas slipped out of his saddle and in two, three seconds Santos lost sight of his shadowy figure. He didn't bother to listen for his movements. No one heard Tomas stalking them until his knife was sawing away at their throats.

Tomas returned as the first shafts of

moonlight began to streak through the thinning clouds. He led Santos and Primitivo through a thick clump of mesquite then down on to the banks of a narrow but free-flowing stream. Several yards beyond the stream Santos could see the dark bulk of a steep butte. He gave a grunted '*Bueno*'. Their rear was protected and he did not doubt that Tomas had found another way out of the thorn barrier. He then gave Tomas further orders.

By the time it was full light, Tomas saw *vaqueros* turning out from their sleeping quarters, a long, low building well outside the compound wall of the don's hacienda, and ride off to relieve the night guards at the herds. The *vaqueros* would present no problem; they would be asleep when he guided Santos and Primitivo into the house. Tomas began to plan out his approach to the hacienda, to remain unseen and unheard by any of the guards. His lips twitched in what passed among his full-blood Yaqui mother's people as a smile. The guards he would have to kill would be beyond all hearing.

★ ★ ★

The major had spent a fitful, sleepless night gazing into the darkness from their cold camp, thinking disturbing thoughts that somewhere ahead of them in this vast Godforsaken land the killers of his sister could be carrying out their bloody business again. And not helping his peace of mind was the throbbing, sickening pain he was suffering from his broken arm. They hadn't seen any *vaqueros*, herds of grazing cattle, nothing that indicated they were riding across Don Argumedo's land before it had got too dark to continue riding.

'I could ride on, Major,' Buckskin had said. 'We can't be that far from the hacienda.'

'It's too risky, Mr Carlson,' the major replied. 'Where Alif and I served anyone caught moving at night was challenged and shot at. Sometimes fired at before they answered the challenge. What little I have seen of this not-so-fair land the same rule applies here. You could run into some of the don's men and be shot down before you could call out that you are a friend. Much against my feelings, Mr Carlson, we will make camp here and move on at first light.' The major looked out into the night for a moment or two before adding, 'And pray that that butcher, Santos, has not yet struck.'

★ ★ ★

As the first glint of the new dawn showed along the eastern horizon, Alif helped a fatigued and pain drawn-faced major into his saddle. Stifling a groan, the major said, 'Now you can press on, Mr Carlson, I am afraid that in the rotten shape I am, I won't be able to ride hard and stay in the saddle.' He managed a weak smile. 'Keep your eyes peeled for any friends of those Indians we had to kill.'

Buckskin grinned back at him. 'Since I hired myself out to you, Major, 'watchful' has been my middle name.' He dug his heels into his horse's ribs and it shot forward in a long, striding gallop.

Within half an hour of leaving the major and Alif, Buckskin came hightailing it back to them yelling, 'There's a bunch of cows away to your left, Major!'

The trail rose steeply and when the major and Alif joined Buckskin on the crest they, too, saw what Buckskin had spotted, cattle and riders coming their way.

'We've made it in time after all, Major,' a joyful Buckskin said. 'The don's crew wouldn't be out tendin' the cows if *bandidos* had raided the hacienda.'

'You could be right, Mr Carlson,' replied the major, hoping with all his being that Mr Carlson's reasoning was correct. The hacienda could be miles away and the *vaqueros* here had not yet heard of any raid.

The dust of the three riders pulling up alongside was still swirling about them when the major asked the *vaquero*, the man whom he knew to be the don's right-hand man, the question he dreaded the answer to.

'Have *bandidos* attacked the hacienda, Señor Zolando?' he said.

Zolando gave the major a surprised look. '*Bandidos* attacking the hacienda, *señor*? I have seen no signs of any such activity and it is only an hour since I left the hacienda.' He favoured the major with a hard-faced smile. '*Bandidos* long ago found it was too costly of their lives to attempt any raids against Don Argumedo's cattle or property, *señor*.'

'Thank God for that!' the major replied. The imperative urgency to keep going and forcing him to control his pain and discomfort had drained away. He sank back in his saddle, exhausted, only his stubborn pride keeping him there.

The major then told Zolando of the killing of two members of the gang who had murdered his sister and how they had found out that the remaining members of the gang, three Mexicans, were planning to raid the don's hacienda.

'We were making all speed to reach the hacienda to warn the don of the threat,' the major said. 'But we had to extract ourselves from a Yaqui ambush, and that delayed us somewhat and cost me a broken arm.'

Zolando narrow-eyed the major. Except for his still steady-eyed gaze, he thought, the Ingles was almost dead in his saddle. The hacienda's straw boss was a hard man, who rarely handed out praise, and hated all whom the Indians called white-eyes, but he was having strong thoughts of respect for this white-eye. He had casually mentioned being jumped by the Yaqui as though it had been of no consequence, except for his broken arm. Zolando wondered how many of the Yaqui ambushers the

194

jefe and his *compadres* had left behind dead. And all done to warn some Mexicans they had only met for a few minutes. Like his *patron*, the don, though slight in build, the Ingles had the balls of a bull.

A sudden disturbing thought put an end to Zolando's assaying of the major's character, and his stoic look changed into one of apprehension. The major seeing Zolando's alarmed expression straightened up in his saddle, once again fighting back his pain and weariness. 'Is there anything wrong, Señor Zolando?'

'It is the Señorita Ortero, *señor*,' Zolando replied. 'Her groom was getting her horse ready for her morning ride when I left the hacienda. She will have two *vaqueros* as escorts, but she could be in great danger if the *bandidos* are watching the hacienda . . . ' His words trailed off. His face twisted in a savage mask. '*Madre de Dios!*' he muttered. 'I must ride to the hacienda pronto, *señor*,' he said. He turned to one of his men and barked out orders. 'Sancho, you ride back to the herd and round up the men and follow me to the hacienda. *Vamos, rapido*! Luis, come with me!'

The straw boss raked his big saw-toothed spurs across his mount's flanks. Rearing and squealing, the horse leapt forward into a hell-for-leather gallop. Luis, wielding his quirt, followed in his dust.

A grim-faced major was thinking of the fate of the young girl if Santos captured her. He gave out his own orders. 'Alif, Mr Carlson, go with the *vaqueros*! I will follow at my own speed.'

★　★　★

Tomas saw the young *señorita* come out of the stables mounted on a grey horse. Then after a few words with an elderly man on the hacienda porch, whom Tomas guessed was the don, she rode out of the compound escorted by two men. Tomas smiled, satisfied. He would be able to give Santos riches without him having to raid the hacienda. The don would part with much of his gold to have the *señorita* returned to him, untouched. If that was too risky a trade, then the Yaqui *jefe* they had dealings with would give them many ponies for a pretty young virgin.

And she would be taken easily. Two well-aimed arrows would dispose of the guards and he noticed that the girl had one of her arms in a sling which would prevent her struggling, save him pistol whipping her and marking her face, lowering her price if she had to be sold to the Yaqui *jefe*. Tomas wormed his way backwards until a fold in the ground hid him from any watching eyes at the hacienda then, getting on to his feet, ran swiftly in a curving path that would get him well ahead of the girl and her escorts and into an attacking position, a swift, silent, killing ground.

The *señorita* Beatrice Ortero rode at a gentle canter. Since the pain of her wounded arm had eased somewhat, she had, much against her uncle's wishes, insisted she would go riding. It was important for her to do so to overcome her still felt fears of her terrible ordeal. After all, she had reasoned, she couldn't stay behind solid walls and armed guards forever. Though when she spoke to her uncle she hid her fears.

'How can there be any danger to me, Uncle?' she had gently chided him. 'I have two *vaqueros* as escorts and I will not be riding more than a mile or so from the hacienda. Then there are *vaqueros* all around me as they ride out to the herds.'

Reluctantly the don had allowed her an early morning ride, but only if she carried a pistol. The pistol he gave her was a small two-load derringer which fitted snugly in the sling strapping her wounded arm to her chest. Beatrice was well aware that her uncle had not given her the pistol to ward off any attack by *bandidos* or Yaqui, but to kill herself rather than be taken alive. A quick death was preferable to the pain and idignity of being a Yaqui squaw or a *bandido's* woman. She didn't try to think too deeply about whether she would have the nerve to put the pistol to her head and pull the trigger if that terrible choice arose.

This was Beatrice's third morning ride and she sat back at ease in the saddle enjoying the cool breeze on her face. Her mind wandered on thinking of how the Ingles major and his fearsome *compadre* were faring in the hunt for the killers of his sister. Beatrice hoped she would see him again. Maybe her uncle would invite him to dinner at the hacienda and he could tell her about London and the other great cities of Europe she had only read about.

A cry of alarm from behind her put an abrupt end to her pleasant thoughts. She twisted round in the saddle in time to see one of her escorts fall off his mount. His *compadre*, who had shouted out the warning, had only time to part draw his rifle from its boot before he too slipped out of his saddle, though time enough for a horrified Beatrice to see the arrow sticking out of his chest before he hit the ground. In a blind panic, she tugged at the reins to pull her mount round to race back to the hacienda and safety. Tomas, gripping the horse's neck, prevented her from doing so.

A wild-eyed Beatrice looked down at the evil-smiling *bandido*. Tomas reached up to drag his prize from the saddle. She felt the touch of his hot hands on her skin as though she was naked. Her worst fears had been realized. That terrible thought broke through her petrified stance, giving her the courage to fight for her life. She let go of the reins and grabbed for the pistol in the sling.

Tomas, who had a Yaqui's hair-trigger reaction to any danger was, for once, caught unawares. The young *señorita*'s beauty and the price she would fetch distracted him momentarily. Eyeing the twin black muzzle holes of a pistol only inches from his face was a stark indication to Tomas that he had suffered a fatal lapse in his behaviour. Then he was beyond any thoughts at all as Beatrice, eyes tight shut, pulled both triggers of the derringer.

Pistol-hand shaking, she opened her eyes to see her attacker falling away from her horse, his face a bloody, featureless mask. Though badly shaken at her killing of the man, Beatrice had still enough control of her actions to get hold of the reins again and kick her heels into her mount's flanks, then, lying low across its neck, rode as fast as she could back along the trail to the hacienda, hoping with all her being that she could stay in the saddle and outride any pursuit.

Constantly looking over her shoulders was proving that her fears were groundless, no one was coming along her back-trail. She straightened up in the saddle and her breathing became more regular. Until, on her left flank, she suddenly saw riders closing in on her. Her fears came flooding back. Then, hardly believing it at first, she recognized one of the leading riders as Señor Alif, the Ingles major's fierce *compadre*. Then she picked out Zolando, her uncle's head *vaquero*. Sobbing with relief, she drew up her horse and mumbled an incoherent thankful prayer to the Holy *Madre* as she waited for saviours to reach her.

Zolando, now at the head of eight riders, had heard the faint popping noise of a firearm discharge and began to curse. It could have only been the sound of the small pistol the *señorita* was armed with. None of his party needed shouted orders to urge their mounts into even greater speed in the direction of where the shots had come from.

The band thundered past the bodies of Tomas and the two *vaqueros*. One rider, at a curt order from Zolando, pulled up his horse to see to their dead *compadres*. The normally hard-assed Zolando favoured Alif and Buckskin with a joyous smile when they saw the *señorita* up ahead seemingly unharmed. The *vaqueros* pulled up in a dust-raising cloud, then drawing out their long guns formed a defensive ring around her.

Beatrice told Zolando of her killing of the *bandido*, which surpised him somewhat, thinking that one of the escorts could have killed him in a last dying action and the *señorita* had only fired her pistol in mad panic.

'You acted like a real *hombre*, *señorita*,' he said. He grinned. 'You have only left two of the dogs for the *muchachos* to kill.'

There were shouts of '*Buenas*, *señorita*' and a '*Shabash*' from Alif when Zolando shouted out the news of the killing of the *bandido*.

Zolando detailed four of the *vaqueros* to escort Beatrice back to the hacienda, then he spoke to the rest of his men. This time his grin had the coldness of death in it. 'Now, *muchachos*, we are going mad-dog hunting. Let it not be said that the young *señorita* is the only *bandido* slayer at the Hacienda La Carendo.' Whoops and howls from the men came in reply to his statement. He looked at Alif and Buckskin. 'You are welcome to join in the hunt, *señors*.'

Alif didn't express his doubts about the wisdom of Zolando's tactics. The remaining two bandits could have seen that their plans of raiding the fine house had gone wrong, that it was time to save themselves from suffering the same fate and that they could be far away by now. If they didn't know things had gone wrong for them, they soon would have suspicions of that, seeing riders searching the land.

The major caught up with them as Zolando was splitting up his men into three groups to widen their search pattern. The straw boss ended the major's worries by telling him that the *señorita* had killed one of the raiders. 'We are now trying to hunt down the other two, *señor*,' he added. 'Soon I will have more men joining in the search.'

The major shot a glance at Alif, noting his sour-faced look. The big Afridi's thoughts about the chances of the *vaqueros* killing or capturing the *bandidos* were the same as his: damn all. As diplomatically as possible, he began to put forward an alternative plan, which, if it worked, could be more successful in avenging his sister's death.

'I admire your intent, Señor Zolando,' he said, 'in trying to catch those killers, but if the *bandidos* have not already departed for safer havens on seeing their comrade killed, they will do so seeing dozens of men quartering the country. They will suspect that something has gone wrong with their plans. So what I suggest is that Mr Carlson and I, seemingly two innocent wayfarers, act as bait to draw them out into the open.' The major smiled at Zolando's raised eyebrows. 'Do not worry, *señor*, we won't be as vulnerable as we look, Alif will be following us on foot, covering us with his Snider.'

Zolando who would bow to no one

when it came to the business of handling cattle, was man enough to admit that the Ingles major, an army man, held sway over him when it came to more-or-less a military operation, small though it may be. Without any argument he said, 'Those dogs killed your sister, Major. It is only right you should lead the hunt to kill them. I will pull back my men but if you should need help, *señor*, three rifle shots will have us riding to your aid, pronto.'

'Good,' replied the major. 'Only one of us is a hero so if we are hard-pressed you'll get your signal, never fear. Of course, we could be doing this all for naught, those bandits could be long gone by now, but I have a strong feeling they are keeping low somewhere in that range of hills behind us. I believe that the man the *señorita* killed had been sent to spy out the land at the hacienda and will not be expected to return at any set time, so two lonely travellers might be too much of a temptation for men who thieve and murder for a living to sit tight and let us pass. If they see no signs of any *vaqueros* they could come out of hiding and try to take us. I am also banking on them not wanting to use firearms so they can't shoot us down from ambush.' He grinned at Alif. 'Mr Carlson and I will be relying on your good eye and equally good aiming.'

Buckskin tried to look unconcerned at acting as a Judas goat even with the 'Dead-eyed Dick' Alif, looking out for him and the major. He had seen the two sons-of-bitches at work. They were mean, ornery, killing *hombres* and were more likely, if they were where the major reckoned they were, to shoot them down from long rifle range than come and hold them up like normal Yankee road agents tend to. Buckskin gave Alif a long meaningful look and he swore the big, Indian-faced giant winked back at him.

★ ★ ★

They were riding on their own, Buckskin resisting the temptation to keep peeking over his shoulder to see if he could spot Alif carrying his big cannon tailing them. Then, finally cursing himself for thinking so loco. If he could see Alif so could the bastards the major and he were hunting, if they were in the hills which were coming blood-chillingly close. The major, Buckskin noted, had the unconcerned look of a man enjoying a leisurely ride. How he could control what he must be feeling getting close to his sister's killers had Buckskin beat.

'We could be riding into dangerous territory, Mr Carlson,' he heard the major say. 'Vigilance must be our watchword. As I told Señor Zolando, if I have surmised right and the men we seek are hiding in yonder hills, and they take the bait, they will not use firearms. Gunshots would give their presence hereabouts away.' He smiled thinly 'After all they are after bigger game than two travellers. They will come in close with cold steel, as the bandits Alif and I fought on our frontier, and with some success I might add.'

Buckskin was wound up as tight as an eight-day clock and a jack-rabbit running across the trail would have him yanking out his pistol and blazing away. This time he couldn't prevent himself from having a reassuring look behind him.

★   ★   ★

'Primitivo!' Santos called out. He was on watch at the edge of the barrier of mesquite and brush, Primitivo was watering the horses at the stream.

'Is it Tomas returning?' Primitivo asked, as he came up to Santos.

Santos shook his head. 'Tomas will not come back until he knows the movement of every *vaquero* at the hacienda. It is two riders who are heading this way. See.'

Primitivo eased himself past Santos until he had a clear view of the riders.

'They look like gringos to me, *jefe*,' he said. He favoured Santos with a surprised look. 'But why would gringos ride this far south?'

Santos shrugged. 'They could be *mal hombres* like us, *compadre*, fleeing from those Texas Ranger dogs. They often cross the Rio Bravo in pursuit of wanted gringos. But they are riding high-stepping horses and we could need extra mounts to carry the riches we will take from the don's grand house. Let us go, *amigo*, and ask those two gringos for their horses.' He gave a death's-head grin. 'While they are dying.'

Though the major and Buckskin were all keyed up expecting trouble the attack came as a complete surprise. The first thing the major knew that his opinion regarding the whereabouts of the *bandidos* had been proved right was when a squat-built Mexican leapt at him from a clump of brush he wouldn't have believed thick enough to have hidden a dog let alone a man. Only the major's quick reflexes, honed fine after years of active service, saved him from death.

Wildly he yanked his horse sideways with his good arm away from his attacker. Primitivo's knife thrust, aiming to deal a killing blow between the gringo's ribs, only plunged deep into his victim's thigh. Primitivo never got the chance of a second strike. Alif's shot tore open his throat in a fearful gush of blood, killing him dead before he dropped to the ground.

Alif was standing in the open, ramming another load into the chamber of the Snider, cursing loudly at not being quick enough to prevent the major from being attacked.

Santos, getting set to jump the elderly gringo, heard the shot and saw Primitivo go down. He cursed as he sank lower into the brush. They had seen two gringos, he thought frantically, now there were at least three. He smelt a trap and had a sudden gut feeling that the reason Tomas had not yet shown up was, like Primitivo, he was dead. He no longer thought of how easy it was going to be to get hold of two horses. It was quitting time if he didn't want to end up as dead as his *compadres*. He began to edge backwards through the brush, keeping the two gringo riders between him and the tall *hombre* with the long gun coming towards them.

Buckskin did his stint of cursing and dirty-mouthing. How could he and the major ride into a stinking two-man ambush like a couple of greenhorn dudes? Out of the corner of his eye, he could see that the major was still in his saddle and he had heard no shot other than Alif's so, if the major was wounded it had been done with a knife, though not serious enough to unseat him. He couldn't see the body of the *bandido* but he had no doubts that following the lump of lead Alif's big gun had fired he was winging his way to Hell. Now it was up to him to make his kill.

With his pistol drawn and cocked, eyes popping in concentration, he scanned the scattered clumps of brush around him for any sign of the second ambusher. A patch no more than fifteen or twenty feet ahead of him swayed as though caught by a sudden gust of wind.

Buckskin didn't hesitate; he was in a killing mood. It could be the wind, but it wasn't the time to take chances. He pulled off three rapid shots into the brush. One of the shells nicked Santos's shoulder, painfully drawing blood. It forced him to realize that he wasn't going to be able to sneak out of this tight corner. If he wanted to make it to his horse he had to kill the old gringo before the Yankee son-of-a-bitch up on his horse could see him and fire a killing shot. Or keep him pinned until the killer of Primivito with his deadly rifle came up. The other gringo wasn't a threat to him. Primitivo had done him a favour before he was killed, by wounding the gringo.

Buckskin saw the last *bandido* rise out of the ground like a latter day Lazarus. The last time he had seen that face he had been a drunken bum watching a bloody massacre, but he would never have forgotten those cruel features even if he had still been hitting the bottle. Buckskin's face twisted into a triumphant smile.

'That ugly sonuvabitch is Santos, Major!' he yelled, as he fanned off the remaining loads in his pistol at Santos.

Santos managed to trigger off one ineffectual shell before feeling real agonizing pain this time, as his left elbow was shattered by one of Buckskin's hastily aimed shots. He lost his grip on his pistol and it dropped to the ground. Sobbing and cursing and holding his wounded arm, he turned and ran, heedless of the spear-sharp spikes of the mesquite tearing at his face and hands, to escape a shell in his nerve-cringing back from the heavy rifle that had killed Primitivo, or a killing shot from the gringo dog who had crippled him.

An anxious-faced Alif reached the major and Buckskin. 'Go and get the bastard, Alif, I'll see to the major!' Buckskin called to him. 'He ain't armed, I busted his gun arm!'

Alif hesitated, looking up at the blood-drained face of his major swaying in his saddle. Then the major became all soldier, as though he was serving on his own frontier. 'Seek him out and kill him, Naik Alif Khan,' he ordered firm-voiced. 'Then the *Pakhtunwali* of the Rifles will not have been violated.'

Buckskin always thought Alif was a frightening-looking *hombre*, but as the big man slung his rifle over his shoulder and drew out his great-bladed knife he saw a face that would scare the hell out of a charging bull buffalo.

Santos burst through the mesquite, clothing slashed, flesh bleeding, as though he had been hacked by knives. His hatred of the gringos who had killed his *muchachos* overcame his fear and pain. He had a spare pistol in his saddle-bags and before he would ride out by the escape route from the camp he would shoot the first gringo who came through the mesquite. His hatred didn't make him loco enough to take on an unknown number of gringos. He was splashing his way across the stream to the horses when he heard the snort of a horse behind him. He stopped in midstream and spun round, hand clutching at his knife, expecting to see the old gringo who had wounded him. Instead he saw six Apache on tail-swishing ponies grinning at him.

Santos's fears took over again. The nerve ends in his wounded arm jumped in even greater paroxysms of pain and he was too dry-mouthed even to curse at how fate, in a matter of minutes, had changed his fortunes for ever. The gringos' bullets would have brought him a less painful death. He gazed desperately about him for the slightest chance of escape, and failed to see one. He just stood there, teeth bared in a defiant snarl like a cornered wolf, waiting for the Apache to dismount and sieze him and begin to torture him.

Instead they just sat there watching him.

Through blood-pounding ears, Santos heard one of the Apache say in Spanish, 'I am Gokilya, known to you Mexicans as Geronimo, a bitter enemy of your people and the gringos, but I will not kill you. A great killing *hombre* will soon have that pleasure.'

Santos couldn't make sense of what he had just been told. He was about to be killed by a 'great killing *hombre*'? Greater even than the bloodthirsty Geronimo whose warband terrorized every village in northern Mexico?

Alif stepped into the clearing, face cut and bleeding as though he had just fought in a battle. Santos took in the tall, hawk-nosed *hombre* dressed in a style he had never seen before — and the fearsome knife he held in his right hand. His defiant lip-curling look froze. He was gazing at the 'great killing *hombre*'. Everywhere he looked, Santos could see only death. He began to sob.

Geronimo spoke again, this time in

English. 'We saw that Mexican dog and a *compadre* lying in wait to kill your *jefe* and the old gringo. We watched you make your kill with your long gun so our help wasn't needed. We have held him here for you to kill. There is a saying among my people that a man would be a fool if he left a live enemy behind him.'

'It is said among my people, Chief Geronimo,' Alif replied, 'that it is not wise to leave a live enemy in front of you.' He strode across to Santos, the sun glinting off the knife blade as he raised it shoulder high.

Santos suddenly snapped out of his fear-induced trance. Mad crazy, howling like a wild dog, he rushed at the 'killing *hombre*', slashing at the air with his knife. Alif, for a man of his bulk, could move swiftly. He stepped to one side, avoiding Santos's stabbing thrusts and, as he charged past him, he gave a grunt and brought down the Kabuli blade in a chopping blow at the back of Santos's neck, almost severing his head from his body. It was a dead man who ran the few paces to the bankside before crumpling to the ground.

The Indians began to talk among themselves. It was a killing that would be talked about at many camp-fires. The manner of the killing brought much pleasure to Geronimo. He had seen the twin of his knife doing its bloody work with great ease. 'You have honoured me with a *bueno* knife, *amigo*,' he said, a smile cracking his deep-lined face. He barked out an order and with a slight swirling of hoof-raised dust, rode out of the clearing.

Alif took one last look at the dead Santos, his blood a lengthening red streak in the water. It had been an easy kill, one an Afridi boy could have managed. But the honour of the Rifles had been redeemed. He wiped his knife clean in the stream before making his way back through the mesquite.

Buckskin, finishing tying a thick pad of bandages round the major's leg wound, saw Alif come into the open. 'The big fella ain't lookin' joyous, Major,' he said. 'I reckon Santos musta hightailed it before he could work on him with that carver of his.'

The major was still up on his horse, feeling like death itself, If he dismounted he would never get back into the saddle. He smiled wanly at Buckskin. 'Mr Carlson,' he said. 'Alif thinks it's a weakness to show satisfaction at doing an everyday task, killing an enemy. Santos is dead, or he would not be strolling towards us.'

The major gave Buckskin a 'told you so' grin at Alif's curt, 'It is done, Major *sahib*.' Sighing deeply he sank back in his saddle. Jennifer could rest in peace. 'Mr Carlson,' he said, 'I never thought that this' — he smiled — 'this mad-assed venture we embarked on would be resolved in our favour.'

Buckskin grinned back. 'I never thought I'd stay sober for so long without goin' crazy, Major. Now, let's get you to the don's place; you're in no fit state to stand another camp in the open.'

'Carry on, Buckskin,' the major replied stern-faced. 'You are the hired guide. It is your task to find our campsites.'

12

Alif sat with his back up against the hacienda wall cleaning and oiling the stripped-down Snider, his big knife stuck in the ground at his side. Standing watching him at work, wide-eyed with curiosity, was a young Mexican boy.

Alif felt at ease in this dry, hot, windswept land. A hill man could breathe here. He felt akin to the *vaqueros*. Sturdy fighting men with a fierce loyalty to each other and the man whose salt they ate. And the women! Alif's stone-hard eyes softened. They were as proud bearing and plump-fleshed as Afridi women. Some bold enough to cast him sultry-eyed gazes as inviting as Kashmiri *houris*.

From the hacienda porch, he heard the major laughing as he talked to the young maiden of the house, something he hadn't heard since the major had been given the grim news of the slaying of his sister. Then came the girl's lighter laugh. There was a time for killing, Alif knew, and a time for pleasure. The major had had a full life of killing; it was his time for pleasure.

The young maiden had seen to the dressing of the major's wound and broken arm when they had ridden in with the news that the *badmash* who had attacked the girl were all dead. Now that the major could walk about with the aid of a stick she accompanied him, arm linked through his, telling him that once his wound had healed they could go riding together. And the major replied how he would look forward to that. It seemed, Alif thought, that they would be staying at this place for some length of time.

Carlson *sahib*, a man he counted as a good comrade, had left to return to his own people. Refusing payment from the major for his services, he had said that the honour of riding alongside the major was payment enough. It was time, Alif thought, he made friends.

He smiled at the lithe-limbed, brown-skinned boy. He could be looking at an Afridi boy. He beckoned for him to sit down. The boy flashed white teeth in a broad grin and lowered himself to the ground. He then picked up a cloth and began to clean the barrel of the Snider.

'*Shabash*,' Alif said approvingly.

THE END